I0705900

Mary and Bright

Nikki Perry & Kirsty Roby

1st edition, 2024

Edited by Eva Chan

Copyright © 2024 in text: Nikki Perry and Kirsty Roby

Nikki Perry and Kirsty Roby assert the moral right
to be identified as the authors of this work.

This is a work of fiction. Names, characters, businesses, places,
events and incidents are either the products of the author's
imagination or used in a fictitious manner. Any resemblance to actual
persons, living or dead, or actual events is purely coincidental.

All rights reserved. Except for short extracts for the purpose
of review, no part of this book may be reproduced, stored in a
retrieval system or transmitted in any form or by any means,
whether electronic, mechanical, photocopying, recording or
otherwise, without prior written permission from the publisher.

No AI Training: Without in any way limiting the author's [and
publisher's] exclusive rights under copyright, any use of this
publication to "train" generative artificial intelligence (AI)
technologies to generate text is expressly prohibited. The author
reserves all rights to license uses of this work for generative AI
training and development of machine learning language models.

ISBN 978-1-9911972-7-6 (paperback)

ISBN 978-1-9911972-8-3 (Epub)

Cover design and layout by Yummy Book Covers

Typeset in PT Serif, 10pt

*For the Grinches and
the Christmas lovers alike.*

They err who thinks Santa Claus comes down the chimney;

he really enters through the heart.

Paul M Ell

Acknowledgements

Thank you so much for reading *Mary and Bright*. If you enjoy the book, *please* consider leaving us a review.

If you would like to read more of our work, you can find out about our other books here:
www.nikkiperryandkirstyroby.com

Thank you to Eva Chan for the copy-editing and to Yummy Book Covers for the gorgeous artwork and formatting.

Mary and Bright

Mistletoe (Viscum album) is from the Anglo-Saxon word misteltān, which means 'little dung twig' because the plant spreads through bird droppings.

Bright

There was bird shit on the windscreen of his dad's 1971 Ford Thunderbird. It was jarring, like seeing Harry Styles with a beer gut. Bright had to look twice to make sure he wasn't imagining it. It was odd enough that the car was parked out on the footpath, but for it to be dirty was something he had never seen. His father had always cleaned that car weekly, polishing it until Bright and Bern could see their almost matching faces in the reflection of the bumper as kids. That car was his father's pride and joy. Bright felt a churn of apprehension in his gut, hurrying up the path to Klaus's house, anxious to make sure his father was okay.

"Dad?" he called, knocking on the front door and testing the handle. It opened easily, the retirement village generally so safe that barely any of the residents ever locked their doors. "Dad, it's Bright, are you here? Is everything okay?"

Inside it all seemed fine; breakfast dishes in the sink, a newspaper open on the bench, the radio playing quietly in the background. Holly the cat looked up from where she was lying on the couch and then, finding nothing worth getting up for, closed her eyes and went back to sleep.

"Klaus?" he tried.

His father emerged from down the hallway, dusting off his pants and smiling widely.

"Hello, this is a nice surprise. I was just thinking about you." He pulled off his wire-rimmed glasses, tucking them into his shirt front, and reached out to give Bright a hug. He smelt of sandalwood, his white grey beard soft against Bright's arm as he pulled away. "Shall I put the jug on?"

"Umm, sure. Why is the Ford parked outside?"

"Huh? Oh. Right. Is it?" Klaus didn't turn to look at Bright, instead pulling out cups from a cupboard and then opening the fridge door to retrieve the milk.

"Dad, you know we talked about you driving," Bright said, opening up the kitchen junk drawer and rustling around. "Do you remember what the doctor told you? You know I'm happy to drive you to the shops any time you want to go. Where are the keys? I'll put it back in the garage for you."

"*No!* " Klaus said loudly, turning and shaking his head.

"No, no, that's okay, it's fine out there," he added more quietly. "Anyway, I forget where the keys are."

Klaus had started to have some issues about a year ago. Little things, like losing his wallet, forgetting how to check his phone for messages, buying cat food and then doing it again the next day until he had months' worth of cat biscuits in the pantry that Holly would, at sixteen, probably never finish in her lifetime. The doctor had confirmed mild dementia, and Bright had been relieved that his father was already in the retirement village, so no major life changes had been necessary.

Even more helpful that he and his brother owned the place and Klaus had been more than happy to move in when it was built ten years ago, despite being the youngest resident at the time. Klaus had been on his own for quite some time by then, and he liked the company of the other residents. Having the memory issues caused no major changes for him. There were already people in place within the community ready to help with health checks, meals and day-to-day care. Except for the car. Several minor prangs had made it clear that Klaus's driving days were at an end, and they had finally agreed that it was best he surrender his licence. He had refused to give up the car though.

"Well, they must be here somewhere," Bright said. "I'll have a look."

"No, no, it's fine. I'm sure they'll turn up soon enough."

"They're probably on the hook in the garage." Bright headed down the hallway to have a look. Klaus stood up quickly, knocking over his seat in the process and startling Holly.

"No, no, don't worry about it, I'll have a look later. Come and have your tea or it'll get cold."

"It'll only take a minute," Bright said, turning the knob on the garage door. It was locked, which was odd.

"I said *leave it*!" his dad shouted down the hallway. "There's no need to treat me like a bloody child."

"Okay, okay, sorry." Bright went back to the kitchen. "It's locked anyway. Have you lost the key to the garage as well?"

"Must have done." Klaus fished out the teabags with a spoon. "Now, do you want milk and sugar?"

"Yes, please." Bright bit back the sadness that his dad could no longer remember how he took it. His mum had died when he and Bern were fifteen and his dad had brought them up alone after that. Every time he forgot something about them, it was a little silent heartbreak.

"What brings you over anyway?" Klaus asked. "Isn't it Monday? You usually come on Fridays, don't you?"

"I'm going to be here every day for a few weeks, while Andrew is away on his paternity leave. I'm filling in as manager." He didn't add that he'd told his dad that several times already. "It was supposed to be next week, but ... anyway, hopefully the timing works out, since we shut down for the holidays at Dainty Dwellings next week."

Bright and his brother had invested in Pacific Palms retirement home together, but after Bern moved to Australia,

Bright had also opened another company, making and selling tiny homes — a market that was steadily increasing and that he knew he was going to need to expand or sell in the near future.

"Right, right, so you'll be up at the office then? All week?"

"Well, daily, although I might have to come and go a bit. But I'll be able to pop in a bit more and say hello."

His dad took a sip of his tea and gave him an odd look. If Bright didn't know better, he'd have thought he looked a bit put out. But he and his dad were close, so he was sure it wasn't annoyance. He took a sip from his own cup and winced.

"Jesus. What the hell sort of tea is this? Is it herbal? It tastes like toenails." He stood and looked at the packet. 'Slippery Elm,' he read. 'Relieves constipation and other stomach ailments.' Bloody hell, he thought, no wonder it tasted awful.

"Bugger," his dad said. "Should have used my glasses. Where the hell did I put them?"

※

Andrew's office looked out over the bowling green and through the glass windows to the enclosed pool, where half a dozen residents were currently bobbing about holding pale-blue pool weights and doing some sort of aqua aerobics, if he were to guess.

There was a list of projects in progress and items that

needed to be taken care of on the desk pad in front of him and Bright also had emails to sort for his own business, but first he decided to ring Bern and catch him before he left for work.

"Morning," his brother said. "Hang on a minute, will ya? Tate, get that away from the dog's bum, it'll get stuck." There was a clatter of cutlery, rustling of a wrapper and several beeps. "Sorry, how's it going?"

"Better for me than the dog by the sounds of it," Bright said drily.

"Bloody lollipops. Di's mother gave the kids a bag of the things and I've already had to cut two out of the carpet."

"How is Di? And the kids?"

"Yeah, all good. But Di had an early meeting which means I'm on school and kindy drop-off, so I can't talk for long. How's it going?"

"I'm filling in for Andrew at the Palms, so I popped in to see Dad."

"How is the old bugger?"

"The Thunderbird was outside," Bright said, watching with surprise as one of the residents walked past the bowlers and gave them the finger. "It was covered in bird shit."

"You're shi— shimmering me?"

"What?"

"Sorry, I've got little ears listening. Are you serious? Dad never leaves that car outside, and bird shi— poop? Is he getting worse?"

"He seemed okay. But he claimed to have misplaced the keys — to the car and the garage."

"Damn. Still, he's in the right place to lose his marbles, isn't he?"

The bowlers were all standing around talking and gesticulating at the retreating back of the old bloke who'd flipped them off and Bright watched as someone in a candy-pink towel that perfectly matched her hair came over to talk to them. She was young. Too young to be a resident in any case, and her legs were rather shapely.

"Bright?" Bern asked. "You still there?"

"Yes, sorry, you were saying?"

"Only that I assumed you and dad would do your same old Christmas dinner? At the same restaurant?"

"Well, yes, I would imagine so."

Their mother had loved Christmas. When they were kids, she had gone all out for the festive season, but after her death, their father refused to do more than have a meal to celebrate. They didn't do stockings or trees or anything remotely Christmassy.

"It's just Di was saying we haven't been home for a Christmas in years and I wondered ... anyway, we'll probably head down to her parents in Margaret River but I thought I'd better check ..."

"Right, right, no point coming all the way over here for a silly commercial holiday ..." Bright was distracted by this woman who was now going round giving the residents damp hugs and laughing, her head back, something sparkling at her ears. She was tiny, not much over five foot and …

"Right. So I guess I'll talk to you later then? Lucy, where are your shoes? Keep me updated about Dad, yeah?"

"Will do," Bright said, holding back a sigh. Christmas always made him a bit depressed. Sometimes he wished he could go overseas and not be the one responsible for his father and their business while his brother enjoyed life in Perth with a wife who loved him and kids who were relatively cute, and not be alone …

Deciding not to dwell, and to focus on the job at hand, he turned away from the window to look back at the first item on his list.

'Organise residents' Christmas party with Mary — need to find room in the budget?' he read, letting out a sigh.

THE NEWSIE

Join Mary in the pool for a low-impact water aerobics class at 10 am Monday morning. Let's get moving and have some fun!

Do we have any knitters looking for a project? Our lovely manager Andrew and his wife Natalie are expecting two bundles of joy this December and I'm sure they would love some knitting done by our fabulous residents.

Remember, all RSVPs for the annual Pacific Palms Christmas party must be in by December 12th. This includes plus ones. Let Mary know if you have any special dietary requirements, please, folks.

CHAPTER 2

Mary

Mary loved her job. She spent some days taking fitness classes, or helping residents with mobility and physio plans. She came up with group activities, arranged outings and social events as well as transport to medical appointments and meals for those who needed them. It was all done with enthusiasm and genuine fondness for the elderly people she dealt with on a day-to-day basis.

But most of all she was super-excited to organise the annual Christmas party, because Christmas to her was the most magical time of the year. She was full of ideas and good cheer changing out of her togs after aqua aerobics and headed to the clubhouse to discuss her plans with her boss.

Knocking on Andrew's door, she peered in, expecting to see his usual messy red curls and instead found a lanky stranger with a mop of salt and pepper hair, pacing back and forward across the paisley carpet.

"Sorry, hello there. I was looking for Andrew?"

"He's on paternity leave, can I help?" the man asked, turning to look at her, then doing a funny little jolt and dropping the glasses that had been hanging from the corner of his lip. "Oh, it's you," he said cryptically.

"It is," she said, smiling broadly. "Are you Albright Nicols? Andrew mentioned you would be in but I thought it was next week." He was quite a nice-looking guy, if a bit scowly.

"Bright," he said, scowling a teeny bit more.

"Sorry?"

"It's Bright. Only my mother called me Albright. Andrew's wife is on bed rest, so his leave had to be brought forward."

"Poor Nat, I can't even begin to imagine the horror of having twins," Mary said with a grin. He didn't smile back. "Anyway, I'm Mary, the activities coordinator. I was coming in for my Monday morning debrief, but it can wait if you're busy?"

"No, now is fine. Take a seat."

"I couldn't fit it in my bike basket," she joked. He looked at her for a long time, his face impassive, until her smile dimmed and she slunk into a chair in front of his desk.

"I need to talk to you about the Christmas party," he began.

"Yes, brilliant, I have so many fun ideas. Decorations, and the food. A magician. I was thinking maybe a fun cocktail, some games. Who doesn't love Christmas after all, and I had an idea for—"

"I don't," he said, cutting her off.

"Sorry, you lost me, you don't what?"

"Love Christmas," he said, taking a seat himself, his long legs banging into the desk. From the look on his face he was serious. She imagined him to be serious a lot in fact.

"I'm sorry to hear that." Mary tried to look contrite. "I love it myself so I'm more than happy to sort the bulk of the party if it's not your thing?" He looked a little relieved, she thought.

"That would be helpful." He rubbed his hand across his forehead. "There's just the matter of the budget."

"Right, yes, I had a look at last year's budget and it was a little bit of a stretch, wasn't it? There's also the fact that we do have more residents this year, so if we could—"

"I'm cutting it by a third," he said, interrupting her. Surely he wasn't serious?

"You're not serious?" She tried for a little laugh. "Is this a joke?"

"It's not a joke, Ms …? Sorry, I don't know your last name?"

"Star, but Mary is fine."

"There's no money in the budget for frivolous things like Christmas, Ms Star," he said. "As it is I'm borrowing from the maintenance fund, so you'll have to make do."

Mary did some mental calculations in her head. No matter how she worked it, she was struggling with how to provide a Christmas meal and entertainment for all the residents. It was a bit of a dick move. Still, she was sure she could think of something. She could be resourceful, and maybe she could make some of the decorations? She was still mulling it over when Lois knocked on the door.

"Hello there, Mary love, fabulous earrings. I was looking for Andrew. The jukebox in the common area has died again. I was hoping he could call that nice man to come back and fix it."

"Hello, Lois, this is Bright, he's taking over for Andrew for a bit while Nat has the babies."

"Well, hello, young man," Lois said, looking at Bright coyly, head tilted and lips pursed. "Aren't you a handsome one. I'm sure *you* can help me with the jukebox."

Mary laughed under her breath. Was Lois actually batting her eyelashes? Wasn't that just an expression?

"I doubt it's worth fixing," Bright said curtly. "The thing's about sixty years old."

"A spring chicken then?" Mary pulled a whoops-that's-a-bit-awkward face at him to imply that Lois was a lot older. He said nothing, merely looked at her like she was a bit mad.

"Now if that's all?" He looked down at his phone. "I have an appointment at eleven."

"Well, he might be dishy but I'm not sure he's an improvement on Andrew," Lois muttered. Mary had to agree. Normally, she could find good things in anyone, but there was no way of sugar coating it, even for her. Bright Nicols was a Grinch. He may have even heard her say it as she walked out the door.

CHAPTER 3

*'Silent Night' is the most recorded Christmas song
in history. It's had more than 733 different versions
copyrighted since 1978.*

Bright

Janice, Andrew's assistant, was buried under a pile of parcels
when Bright arrived at the village late the next morning.

"Oh good. You can drop these off to your dad for me," she
said, peering out from behind the stack of boxes and several
large courier bags.

"All of them?" Bright asked, dubiously.

"Yep. Looks like someone's going to get lucky this
Christmas."

"I doubt that very much," Bright muttered, but he found
an empty box near the printer and scooped the parcels into
it.

Janice gave him a grateful smile, pushed her glasses onto the bridge of her nose and went back to tapping away on her laptop. "Also, Mr Cartwright is waiting for you in your office. He's been there since nine-thirty," she added, without looking up.

Bright carried the box into his office and found a space for it on top of the filing cabinet. "Good morning, Mr Cartwright," he said to the elderly man, who was glaring up at him from one of the two worn visitor chairs.

"Is this what you call morning? It's almost afternoon. What kind of time is this to be starting work?"

"Well, I do have another business ..."

"Don't give me your excuses, I'm not interested. In my day, a man would have put in several hours of hard labour by now. What are you going to do about my front porch light? Could have broken my neck if I'd been out after dark." He took a sip from a cup perched on the end of Bright's desk. "And this tea is dreadful."

"What exactly is the problem with your porch light?"

"It's not working, is it? It should be in the records. I sent one of those online messages to Mr Stevens last week and nothing has been done about it, which is typical, of course."

Bright quickly brought up Mr Cartwright's file on Andrew's desktop computer.

"Yes, I see you lodged a notice on Friday evening," he said.

"Mr Stevens — Andrew — is away on paternity leave at present so there hasn't been time to action that yet."

Mr Cartwright scoffed. "Paternity leave? What kind of nonsense is that?"

Bright decided to ignore that. "I'll make sure the electrician calls in as soon as possible, Dougal."

"That's Mr Cartwright to you," he huffed, pulling himself to his feet. "I want it done by tonight."

"I'll do my best," Bright said, but Dougal was already shuffling out of the room and, if he heard, he didn't respond.

***

Klaus didn't answer when Bright poked his head through the door to his unit, calling his name, a couple of hours later. He left the box of parcels on the bench and had a quick look around but his father wasn't in the house, or in the small garden. The radio was on, 'Jingle Bells' playing softly. The Thunderbird was still parked in the driveway and when he tried it, the garage door remained locked. He headed back up to the main building where he decided to stop at the cafeteria for a proper cup of coffee. Janice had brought him a cup of tea earlier and Dougal had been right about one thing: it was dreadful.

As Bright waited for his latte, he glanced around and saw his dad sitting at a corner table eating lunch. He took his coffee and went over to join him.

"Well, hello." Klaus beamed up at him. "Is it Friday

already?"

"I'm working here for a bit." Bright eyed the spread in front of his father. A plate with the smeared remains of a chicken pie was pushed to one side and Klaus was eating a blueberry muffin. He also had a cream doughnut and a bliss ball.

"That's a decent lunch, Dad. Maybe I could have a bit of that doughnut?"

Klaus grunted and reluctantly tore off a piece. Bright chewed for a bit and his dad sipped his tea.

"I've been to drop off a stack of parcels to your house," Bright said.

"Good, good." Klaus finished the last of the muffin and tucked into the remaining doughnut.

"There were a lot of them. What are they anyway?"

"Hmmm? This is pretty good. You should get one."

"Dad. The parcels."

"What parcels?"

Bright sighed. "The ones I dropped off at your place. That you had delivered to the office."

"Right, yes. From the internet. Did you know you can get almost anything online these days? Except hay. The young man I spoke to said I should try a pet store."

"Why on earth would you want hay?"

"I'm not saying I do. But if I did, they wouldn't deliver it here."

"Right, well, I'll come down a bit later and have a look."

He wanted to make sure Klaus wasn't losing his marbles. Or being taken advantage of. He and Bern had set up an account so that Klaus had a certain amount of spending money when he'd started to become forgetful — as they liked to phrase it — so there was no risk his dad was whittling away his life savings, but he wanted to find out what, exactly, was going on.

"There's no need to have a look," Klaus said. "It's nothing to do with you. You don't see me poking my nose into your private business, do you?"

"Sorry. I'm just a bit concerned."

"Well, you can bloody well not be. I can take care of myself. I don't suppose you could pick me up a loaf of bread before you come over though, could you?"

Bright stood and patted his dad gently on the shoulder. "Sure, that's not a problem. I'll come by about four."

"Make it four-thirty. I'm pretty busy."

On his way back to the office he passed Mary who was decorating the front desk in the foyer. She was wearing a striped green and white dress and looked like a ridiculous pixie. Bright slunk past not wanting to be pestered by more party details. She was singing a Christmas carol, loudly and out of tune, and Bright thought longingly of his office at Dainty Dwellings, the smell of sawdust and the steady, although slightly gloomy, presence of his business partner Gary.

"No more parcels, Janice?" he asked.

"No more, thankfully. That's the third lot we've had for your dad in as many weeks. I had to send back two pairs of gumboots for him that were the wrong size last week. Has he taken an interest in gardening?"

Klaus had never much liked gardening. That had been his mum's domain. After she'd died, the gardens had gradually turned to weeds and then his dad had removed them and returned it to lawn. They'd had the most boring garden in the street. Grass and a few trees. Plenty of room to kick a ball around though. Now, Klaus's section was maintained by the Palms and it was hardly big enough to need a pair of gumboots. He'd grown up on a farm though, so perhaps he was getting confused and thought he still lived there.

Bright looked through the window at the pool. There was one lone swimmer, doing slow laps. He should take advantage of the facilities — there was a pretty good gym too. At the moment, all he did was work, visit his dad and go for runs. The occasional beer with friends. Anything to avoid his empty house.

THE NEWSIE

Anyone interested in an outing to the reserve on Friday, please let Janice know by Wednesday, thank you.

Lawn bowls members: please remember to put your mallets back in the equipment shed if you have the last game, it is much appreciated.

Did anyone lose a pair of reading glasses on Sunday in the library? Janice has them.

CHAPTER 4

Mary

Mary had strapped on her yellow helmet and was about to hop on her bike for the ride home when Lois appeared from behind an azalea bush, as if by magic.

"I'm glad I caught you," she said, taking dainty little steps in her red silk slippers across the manicured lawn. "Are you able to pop in for a cuppa sometime tomorrow? I'm having a bit of trouble with my swipe thingy and I'd like to call the grandies."

"Ah, your Skype. Yes, of course. Around ten?"

"Lovely." She eyed Mary's pink bicycle wistfully. "I had a bike like that when I was a little girl, but mine was blue with red tassels on the handlebars. My mother would send me down for bread and I'd cycle back with the loaf in the basket, still warm." She gave Mary a pat on the arm. "You take care now, and ride safely. I do worry about you, with all the traffic nowadays."

"Thank you, Lois, I'm very careful, I promise. I'll see you tomorrow."

As she rode she mentally ran through a list of things she needed to do. Cycling was always good for that. A time when she could reflect on the day that had passed or prepare herself for the day to follow. It was almost like her daily meditation and she missed it when the weather was so bad she had to drive her car instead. Tonight there was coconut ice to make and she needed more food colouring and some silver ribbon. Her bathroom needed a good scrub and at some point she wanted to get a tree and decorate her house. She had a big plastic box in the garage with bits and pieces she'd gathered over the years. Many of the decorations dated back to her childhood; things she'd made with her gran or they'd picked up in the post-Christmas sales; or ornaments she'd collected since then. Most were precious or sentimental.

After looking through decorations at the village she'd realised how sparse the collection there was by comparison. They'd lost most of them last year when the tree had toppled over after a stray cat got inside, but she dreaded having to approach Bright about a budget for more. Perhaps she could hold a craft morning and the residents could make streamers and snowflakes. The lounge would no doubt look like a primary school classroom but there wasn't much to do about it if he was going to continue to act like a Grinch.

As she reached the end of the road, a large silver car roared past, straight through a puddle and way too close, splashing muddy water up her legs. She wobbled a bit and was taken aback when the driver had the nerve to give her an aggressive honk. Looking up she saw it was Bright. She was pretty sure he was scowling, even though his face wasn't visible. Resisting the urge to give him the finger — he was her boss, after all — Mary righted herself and watched as he retreated into the distance.

Patsy was waiting for her on her front steps when she pulled into the driveway, her blonde curls springing out from her head in a wild halo. She was wearing denim shorts and a bright-orange shirt, her legs out in front of her, head tilted back and eyes closed. Next to her sat a paper bag, overflowing with tinsel.

"Hello, have you been waiting long? You could have used the spare key, you know," Mary said, dismounting and leaning her bike up against the side of the house.

"I'm enjoying the fresh air, and the key is only for emergencies. I don't want to impose."

"Pats, I've known you for a million years. I wouldn't mind."

"I just popped in on my way home to drop off some Christmas decorations that we had donated today. Thought you might be able to use them at the Palms?" She stood and picked up the bag, letting Mary pass to let them both inside the house. "We get so many in the New Year and no one will want these ones since they're a bit dated. I figured you could work your magic and upcycle them somehow?"

Patsy lived a street over and worked at a charity organisation. She and Mary had been friends since they met there when they both volunteered in high school. Patsy was still there, now managing the place.

"Your timing is perfect," Mary told her. "I'm desperate for Christmas things now I have to deal with Grinchy Bright. Cup of tea? Or a cold drink?"

"Water is fine." Patsy put the bag on the bench and leant against the bench. "Grinchy who?"

"Bright. My new boss. Well, temporary boss. He's a real jerk. He's cut the Christmas party budget into an almost impossible amount. He might be kind of hot but he's a cold fish."

Patsy gave her a questioning look as she took the offered glass of water from her. "He's hot?"

"His hotness is not the point," Mary said. "He's awful, Patsy. He even hates Christmas. I mean, who hates Christmas?"

"Well, if anyone could change his mind about that, it'd be you," Patsy said with a grin. "And best you ignore any hotness anyway if he's your boss. That never ends well."

"True. In any case, how's work?" Mary asked as she got her own drink.

"Busy," Patsy told her, "which is another reason I popped in." She gave Mary a mock, sad frown. "Any chance you could help me deliver some Christmas parcels sometime in the next week or so? Paul's sprained his wrist so he's out of action for any heavy lifting."

"Sure, no problem," Mary said. "Happy to help."

"Thanks, hun, I knew I could count on you."

"That's what friends are for, right? Want to stay for tea? We could get a curry?" Mary suggested.

"Perfect. I never order one for just me. The one peril of being single." Patsy finished her drink. "That and having to take out the rubbish yourself."

Lois must have seen Mary approaching the next morning, as she had the tea cups ready and the kettle on when Mary knocked on her door shortly after ten. There was a small present sitting on the bench, neatly wrapped in red paper with a shiny white bow.

The compact unit was pristine, carpet freshly vacuumed and Lois's collection of china cats gleaming from every possible surface. Her fat, lazy cat, Mr Thomas, was stretched in the sun in front of the open ranch slider and Mary bent to give his belly a rub. She gave Lois a small bunch of lavender sprigs from her garden, tied with ribbon.

"Thank you, love," Lois said, smelling the flowers. "Come and sit up at the counter and chat to me." She poured hot water onto the tea bags. "I've got to finish rolling out this pastry and get it into the fridge." She nudged the present over with her elbow, hands now dusted with flour. "A little something for you, to say thank you for everything you've done for me this year."

"Thank you, Lois, you really didn't have to get me anything. I love helping you out." It was also her job, but Mary really did enjoy helping the residents. "I've got a little something for you too."

"Please tell me it's your fabulous coconut ice?"

"It is." Mary placed one of the cellophane packets onto the bench. "Although, I'm not sure how fabulous it is."

"We all think it's delicious, and that's all that matters. Well, maybe not Dougal, but nothing will make that man happy. Open your gift."

Mary carefully peeled away the paper.

"It's a bell. For your bike," Lois told her, unnecessarily. "I was going to get you earrings but I couldn't find a pair you don't already have."

"No, I suspect I own one of every pair at the two-dollar shop now," Mary said with a laugh. "Thank you, Lois, it's perfect." She thought of Bright, honking at her the night before. "I hope it's a loud one."

Lois lifted her pastry into two small pie tins and neatly cut the edges. "I'm making an asparagus quiche, plus an extra one for Jerry. It worries me that he doesn't take good care of himself." She popped the pastry into the fridge and washed her hands.

"That's very kind of you." Mary wasn't sure whether Jerry

really wasn't the best of cooks or if Lois enjoyed fussing over him. It was true they'd had to call the fire brigade when he'd fallen asleep while making a cheese toastie earlier that year but, since then, Lois cooked twice as much most nights and traipsed over to the other side of the village to deliver him a meal. It was probably where she'd been when she'd popped out of the bushes the evening before.

Lois waved an arm dismissively, as though it really wasn't a big deal. "It's not only me. Glenda made him a Christmas cake although, between you and me, I felt it was a bit dry."

Glenda was their newest resident and Mary was due to call in to see her later that day.

While they drank their tea, Lois showed Mary the most recent photos of her grandsons, who lived in Wales. Lois hadn't met the youngest, who had recently turned four, going a bit misty-eyed at one image where they wore matching 'We love Grandma' T-shirts.

"Shall we have a look at your computer now? I'm sure those lovely boys of yours are hoping for a call," Mary said, as Lois dabbed her eyes with a hanky.

Twenty minutes later Mary left Lois happily chatting to her daughter-in-law and little grandsons and made her way up to the main office.

"Could I see Mr Nicols?" she asked Janice, handing her a package of coconut ice.

"Yum, thank you. Yes, he's in. I'd nab him now before the electrician gets here." Janice pulled open the cellophane and popped a piece of the sweet treat into her mouth.

Mary rapped lightly on Bright's closed door and got a brusque 'Come in'.

He was sitting at his desk, reading something on the laptop, deep frown lines creasing his forehead. He looked up as Mary entered. "Oh, it's you. I was expecting the electrician."

"I only need a moment." She slid a cellophane bag onto the desk. "This is for you."

The frown lines got deeper. Bright handled the bag delicately as though it contained a bomb, or dog poo. "What is it?"

"It's coconut ice."

He pushed it back to her. "No, thanks, I don't eat sweets. I'm sure someone else will appreciate it more."

You'd benefit from it, you sour git, she thought. "I wanted to talk to you about a little extra in the budget for Christmas decorations" is what she said instead.

"Didn't I see you decorating yesterday? And Janice tells me you usually get a tree for the lobby. I'm not sure what else you need."

"Some of the decorations are looking a little shabby so I thought it would be nice for the residents if we replaced them. I'm planning on having a craft session to make the lounge area look festive for the party and I'd like to buy a few supplies for that, before I put a notice in the weekly *Newsie*."

"The what?"

"The *Newsie*. It's a newsletter to inform the residents about what's going on for the week. A little something I started up a few months ago—"

"Of course you did."

Mary ignored the interruption. "And it's very popular."

Bright sighed and rubbed at his temples, like the mere thought of forking out money had given him a migraine. "Okay, get Janice to give you some money from petty cash. No need to go crazy though."

Mary resented that he thought she was going to run out and buy a truckload of Christmas tack. And what exactly did he mean by 'Of course you did'? This man didn't even know her, yet he was acting like he did, and that he didn't like what he saw.

"You're welcome to come and join us, of course. More hands make light work. I imagine you'd be fantastic at rustling up fabulous decorations out of practically nothing," she said sweetly.

Bright turned back to his computer. "Not really my thing, but I applaud your resourcefulness, Ms Star."

"Sure, fair enough." Mary thought for a minute. "I'm taking a group of residents out to see the Christmas lights. Perhaps you would like to come along to that?"

Bright leant back in his chair and looked at her. "I'd rather eat a toenail sandwich," he said. "Anyone's toenails, not even my own."

Mary stood rooted to the spot for a few seconds. Was he serious? His face remained unmoved. Deciding it wasn't worth an argument, she turned and headed for the door, her festive silver bell earrings ringing wildly and not very cheerily.

CHAPTER 5

The custom of bringing evergreens into the home
began in the 16th century as a way of cleaning up
the Christmas tree and making it more uniform.
Instead of throwing out cut-off greens, people wove
the excess into wreaths.

Bright

The woman was ridiculous. With her silly pink hair and tacky earrings. She was tiny. Like a pixie or an elf. And cheerful! Relentlessly cheerful — all sunshine and unicorns. It made him feel old and beige and, for God's sake, why was he still thinking about her.

"... would be the cheapest option if you don't want to go with the full shebang," the electrician finished saying, and Bright realised he hadn't been listening, too busy thinking about that ridiculous Mary with her dimple and her big blue eyes.

"Yes, that sounds like the best way to go," he said, hoping the cheapest option was a good one and too embarrassed to admit he'd drifted off. "Thanks for that, Dave. When do you suppose you'll get it done?"

Dave scratched behind his rather large ear, looking up at the sky like it would give him some clue as to his work calendar.

"How does Monday sound? I'll have to switch things off at the mains, so you might want to let the oldies know in advance."

"Monday would be great. I'll put a note in the *Newsie*," Bright said and then felt like an idiot when Dave gave him a weird look.

"Right, well, I'll be off then. Got a job to get to, down at the mall grotto."

The day dragged on, with Bright trying to sort admin and being constantly interrupted by requests from residents. Somebody had emailed asking if he would be interested in participating in a Christmas parade. He gave them a firm no, along with the emails about Christmas cookies and charity Christmas crackers, and replied no thank you to the staff email about joining in the Secret Santa exchange.

Lois was back asking about croquet clubs and Glenda, a plump woman with a sharp grey bob, arrived with a piece of cake that she insisted he take, despite his protests.

Christmas wreaths now lined the office doors and entryways, the smell of fresh pine making him sneeze and itch.

Right before lunch he spotted Dougal heading up the path and deciding enough was enough, ducked out the fire exit, skirting past the pool to go the long way around to his dad's place.

Klaus was sitting at the kitchen bench, glasses perched on his nose, writing in a notebook. Beside him was an extremely large plate of sandwiches and a glass of milk.

"Are some of those for me?" he asked as he came in the door. "What are they? Ham and cheese?"

His dad did a funny little jump, his hand on his heart.

"Cripes, don't sneak up on a man like that!" He closed the notebook and then put it on his seat and sat back down on top of it, then got up again. "I wasn't expecting you, but I'll make you a plate." He went around to the other side of the bench, opening a drawer and sliding the notebook inside as he did, a cagey look on his face.

"You've got a pretty good pile there already, Dad," Bright said. "I'll have one of those."

"No, I'll make you one. I'm hungry today," his father insisted, pulling out bread and opening the fridge.

"What's with the notebook?" Bright asked, getting himself a plate from the cupboard.

"Just making a list," Klaus said vaguely, "Is it Friday?"

"No, it's Thursday."

"I thought you came on Fridays?" Klaus said, pulling out a jar of apricot jam.

"I'm working up at the office for a bit," Bright told him, trying to be patient. He put the jam back in the fridge and got out the pickle. "Andrew is away."

"Who's Andrew?" Klaus asked, his forehead furrowed.

"The manager here, Dad."

"I'd better put him on my list," Klaus said. "Do you want a sandwich?"

The weekend dragged by slowly. He'd done his laundry and a food shop and weeded the garden and it was only Saturday afternoon. When Gary rang to see if he wanted a game of golf, he was quick to agree.

They played nine holes and then went for a drink. The weather was getting warmer and the beer tasted bloody good. Bright eyed up the bowl of nuts on the table, trying to decide if he wanted to order food.

"How's it going with all the oldies anyway?" Gary asked, wiping the back of his neck with his napkin. "Christ, it's hot, my balls are like roast spuds in butter."

He might pass on the food, Bright decided.

"It's fine," Bright said. "It'll be easier now we've shut down for the holidays."

"I'm happy about the Christmas bonus by the way," Gary said. "Appreciate you sorting the books. Means I can get the kids something a bit more exciting from Santa this year."

"No worries." Bright took a long gulp of his beer. "Are you going away at all?"

"Yeah, off camping over New Year's on a mate's property. He's got one of those lifestyle blocks. Keeps a few goats, a couple of ponies for his kids, that sort of thing. Even has a llama." He drained his beer and raised the empty at Bright. "Another one?"

"Sure."

"Cor, look at the rocks on that bird's ears," Gary said as he stood to go to the bar. Across from them, a rail-thin woman in a white monogrammed golf shirt was sitting, designer sunglasses perched on her head and the light hitting the side of her face where a mammoth cluster of diamonds sparkled. "Bet she's high maintenance," Gary added, "just your type." He sloped off with their empties. Bright sat and watched the woman, her red lips pursed in disgust at something the man opposite her was saying.

She was the polar opposite of Mary, he thought, with her silly dollar-shop earrings and her ready smile. And dammit; why was he still thinking about her?

❄

He turned up to Pacific Palms on Monday feeling rather odd. His stomach was acting up a bit, he thought, like the time when Bern had made him bungee jump and he'd stood on the edge of the Kawarau bridge and belatedly remembered that he didn't much care for heights. Or when he used to get excited about Santa as a kid.

Janice had left him a note to say she had an appointment and wouldn't be in until lunchtime but that he'd find a list of residents' issues on his desk. Whoever had come up with the idea of a complaints box was the bane of his life. He took the stack of notes and then a piece of coconut ice from its cellophane wrapper, popping it in his mouth without thinking. He didn't normally indulge in sweets but he had to admit, it was delicious.

He sorted through some emails first, deleting anything that looked like spam and earmarking anything that Andrew would need to do from home. Someone had put on music, he realised, when he found himself horrified to discover he was singing along to 'Snoopy's Christmas'.

He started on the complaints. A resident had found a bag of rubbish in their bin that wasn't theirs. Someone else thought the happy hour was getting too raucous and needed to start earlier so that the 'shenanigans' would be done by four. There was a complaint about a barking dog, one about how many lawn ornaments were allowed, one about inappropriate use of the personal alarms, and one from Dougal — he'd signed his — complaining about the 'stupid bloody meditation class'. According to him, the humming was too loud and it put him off his chess game.

Bright quite liked a game of chess, and he could sympathise on being distracted. It was, after all, a very intellectual game. But he found it hard to imagine a meditation group could be *that* noisy.

A quick check showed the class was scheduled on Mondays at eleven. He glanced at his phone. Eleven-fifteen. Might as well have a look. Or listen.

In the rec room, he found a gaggle of senior women in a sea of pastel leggings and cotton shirts, and one lone man in running shorts and singlet, sitting on chairs with their eyes closed, hands on their knees, palms up.

Mary was facing them, her pink hair boosted upright by a neon-yellow sweatband, a pair of snowmen dangling from her ears. She was wearing a pair of denim shorts and a top with a cartoon avocado on it — the words 'avo cardio' written underneath.

She was very distracting, but Bright could still hear the dreadful noise they were all making. It was like a herd of cows waiting for milking, all lowing and oom-ing, and, for some reason, Bright found himself laughing. Out loud.

THE NEWSIE

A reminder that the power will be off for a brief period at 10 am and we apologise for any inconvenience this may cause.

Meditation class is on again in the rec room at 11 am on Monday. All welcome.

A gentle reminder too that rubbish bins are provided for each unit — please respect this and keep to your own bin.

CHAPTER 6

Mary

He was rather gorgeous when he laughed, Mary noted. Smiling changed his face and his eyes sparkled. He had lovely even white teeth too and his laugh was deep and rumbling.

Still, it was a bit rude, coming into a meditation session, where everyone was in their own zen space, and interrupting things.

"Can we help you?" she asked, gritting her teeth a little.

Lois's eyes popped open. "Hello there, Mr Nicols. Why don't you come and join us?" She hopped up as though to get him a chair, moving way more quickly than you'd think possible of a woman nearing eighty.

"Not today, Lois. I'm not really dressed for it."

"I'm sure you'd find it very relaxing. Mary's an excellent teacher."

"No doubt." He cleared his throat. "Although there has been a small complaint. About the humming."

"Sorry?" Mary wasn't sure she'd heard him right. "The humming?"

"Yes. It's quite loud. And distracting. Apparently."

"That's unfortunate," Mary said. "Perhaps we could try chanting instead?"

"There's no other room you could practise in?" The tips of his ears flushed a little pink.

"Well," Mary cast her hand around the space, 'this *is* the rec room. Would you prefer we used the movie theatre? Or maybe outside, on the lawn?"

"I mean ... it's not like I'm the one who made the complaint ..."

Mary was fairly certain she knew who did.

"Perhaps the chess players could reconvene to the craft room or the library if the noise was bothering them? I believe it's usually free at this time." She tried to keep her face neutral and not give way to the grin that was threatening to break out.

Bright's head turned quickly towards the door and then back and Mary guessed her suspicion about who had made the complaint was correct.

"Right," he said. "I'll pass that on."

"There's a CD player in the cupboard, and I believe a selection of classical music. Maybe André Rieu would block out the sound of our humming?"

The deep lines that had appeared between Bright's eyes relaxed. "Excellent idea, Ms Star."

Mary hopped up and crossed to the cupboard where she easily found the portable CD player and handed it to Bright. His skin was warm where their fingers brushed. She didn't know why that surprised her. It wasn't as though his hands would be icy cold in summer.

"Mary," she said.

"Pardon?"

"Please call me Mary, not Ms Star."

"Mary," he mumbled. "Thank you for your cooperation."

"My pleasure."

Mary finished off the class and then went down the hall to the library where she had left her bag. She had a small, usually empty room there that was both her office and an internet area for the residents and she used it to type out her newsletter and do her planning for any outings and activities.

She thought about Dougal Cartwright as she sat there. He was always extra grumpy at this time of year. Her first year here she had been keen to make him a little less miserable, but, try as she might, she'd not succeeded. She knew better now than to try to befriend him.

Her grandmother had always said that 'one happiness scatters a thousand sorrows' and, in most cases, Mary found this to be true, but Gran had also told her 'the memory of happiness makes misery woeful', and this summed up her experience of Dougal. He seemed so regretful of all he had lost, unable to move on.

He'd been married a long time ago, until his drinking had forced his wife to leave, taking his small daughter Rachel with her back to England. Dougal had had no contact with them after that, except to send money to Rachel's Bonus Bond account, until one year he discovered it had been closed. Rachel sent him a Christmas card every year, and that was all he had left of his family. It was extremely sad.

Her own parents had been awful, her early years unpleasant, but after she was moved to her gran's 's custody, life had been wonderful for Mary. She felt very lucky to have had someone who loved her so unconditionally. She doubted Dougal had ever had that.

She thought about Bright as she tried to juggle the budget for the party, and wondered if he had something in his past that made him the way he was. She needed to try to befriend him, she decided. He might be grumpy, but she was sure that deep down, he was a nice guy.

❄

"You took those from Jerry," someone said outside her door.

"They were left there for me," a man replied. "They're mine."

"I left them there for Jerry."

"Well, how was I supposed to know that?"

"Because they were on his front doorstep."

Mary got up and poked her head into the library. Klaus

stood, one arm extended, a plate perched above his head. In the other hand he held a half-eaten biscuit. Glenda stood in front of him, hands on hips. She was a diminutive woman, wearing sensible shoes and a string of pearls, but she looked like she was ready to tear strips off Klaus like a rabid Rottweiler.

"You give them back right now. They're my famous raisin and oatmeal biscuits and I baked them especially for Jerry, not for you."

"Well, I assumed they were for me," Klaus said, taking another bite. "Why would you make Jerry cookies?"

Glenda went a bit pink. "Never you mind. The fact is, you've stolen his baked goods."

"I'm sure this is all simply a bit of a misunderstanding," Mary said, "Perhaps if Klaus could have the one he's started and then I could drop the rest off to Jerry?"

Klaus lowered his arm. "Well, I might have had more than just this one already," he told her a bit sheepishly. There were only two biscuits left on the plate.

"You … you …" Glenda gave him a death stare. "You big guts."

Klaus beamed as if she'd given him a compliment, handed her back the plate and waltzed out of the room, patting his belly.

"Well, I never," Glenda said. "Poor Jerry, I'll have to make another batch. Only that was the last of my golden syrup, blast it all."

"I'm happy to pop down and get you some more if you need it," Mary offered. Glenda gave her a grateful smile. "Would you, love? That would be wonderful."

"No problem."

"Actually, could I give you a little list?" Glenda said, passing Mary the plate so she could reach into her handbag and pull out a spiral-bound notebook and pencil. She wet the end of the pencil with her tongue and started to write.

"Just some raisins, a bag of sugar, butter, some bananas, but not if they're too ripe, maybe some ice cream if they have that nice rum and raisin one ..."

Mary removed a biscuit off the plate and took a bite. It was delicious.

THE NEWSIE

We have an outing planned for Saturday afternoon to the art gallery if anyone is interested in attending. Please see Janice for details.

Also on Saturday, there will be Christmas movies playing in the theatre.

10 am Love Actually

2 pm Home Alone

6 pm The Holiday

CHAPTER 7

Mary

Briar Farley reminded Mary of a cartoon rabbit. She wore her hair in two short ponytails that flopped either side of her head and her front teeth were large. As the manager of the village kitchen, she was in charge of the Palms cafe food. She and Mary sat at one of the cafe tables to discuss the Christmas party menu.

"The biggest issue," she told Mary as she poured them each tea, "is that the staff would need to be paid double time to work Christmas Day, since we are contracted by the village and not owned by them. That's if you could persuade them to work in the first place."

"With the budget being cut, I don't think that's going to be an option," Mary sighed. "Is there any way you could prep food and I could do the cooking on the day?"

Briar thought it over for a bit. "I mean it's doable, but it's a big job." She sipped her tea. "What we could do is make you some nice salads. They'd only need dressing. And do a cold ham?" She passed Mary over the plate of shortbread and then took one for herself. "If you could handle the turkeys, you could just have roast potatoes with it. We could probably prep those for you at no cost and we could whip up some pavlovas? They're fairly cheap to make." She bit into the biscuit and chewed. "You'd need to decorate them in the morning," she said around a mouthful.

"I could do that," Mary said. "What about the Christmas puddings? We'd need at least three."

"Oooh, now they're pricey." Briar wrote down some more numbers on the pad beside her on the table. "That's going to tip you right over budget. Could you make those? They can be done well in advance."

"I guess." Mary was starting to feel a bit overwhelmed, but what else could she do?

To say thank you for doing her shopping, Glenda had invited Mary for morning tea. She turned up at ten with some parsley from her garden, since there had been none at the shops when she'd gone down to get the long list of requirements and Gran had always said you never turn up without a gift for the hostess.

Glenda lived in one of the units at the edge of Pacific Palms, overlooking the estuary. Beside her front door was a large ornamental figure of a butler holding out a tray. The doormat read 'Welcome to the nut house'. Mary knocked, taking off her sandals as she waited.

"Well, hello there, doll," someone said and she looked up to find a man standing there, dressed in a pair of basketball shorts and a T-shirt with a Guns N' Roses logo on it. He had several piercings in one ear and an almost mullet.

"That'll be Mary," she heard Glenda calling from inside. "Hello, love, come on in." Glenda appeared, motioning to Mary. "This is Dallas, my gorgeous grandson. Dallas, this lovely young lady is Mary, our village angel that I was telling you about."

"You didn't mention what a stunner she is, Nan," he said, giving Mary a cheeky wink.

"Oh, he's incorrigible," Glenda laughed. "Dallas, come and have a look at this jug, will you, and we'll have a cuppa and a piece of my famous lemon slice." She gave Dallas an affectionate pat on the arm. "It's the oddest thing, Mary — every time I try to boil the jug, the kitchen lights turn on or off."

"We might have to crack open a bottle of wine instead, Nan," Dallas suggested. "Or shall we do that later, Mary? I could buy you a drink and you could show me around while I'm in town."

On her way back to the clubhouse, full of tea and lemon slice, Mary was surprised to discover Klaus leaning a long ladder up against one of the residents' houses. He began to climb up and she rushed over to stop him.

"Mr Nicols, wait." She tried to keep hold of his arm and the ladder. "Whatever are you doing?"

"Checking the chimneys," Klaus told her with an exasperated roll of his eyes.

"Well, I'm sure that's not necessary. The maintenance crew check them annually in May to make sure they're all good for winter. You really shouldn't be up ladders at your age."

"No good in winter," he said, trying to take a step up the first rung. "It needs to be done now. I can see this one from my place and there's a bird's nest up there that needs to be cleared."

"Well, I can't have you up there," Mary insisted. "Do you know how many elderly people fall off ladders?"

"Can't be helped," Klaus shrugged, taking another step up.

"Oh, my goodness, your son will shoot me," Mary muttered. "All right, all right, I'll do it. Please, get down. You can hold the ladder."

Klaus stepped back down and Mary started tentatively up the ladder, the side of the house now seeming much taller than it had from the ground. She wasn't that keen on heights, she remembered about halfway up.

"Dad? Mary? What on earth?" There was a large hand on her ankle and she looked down to see Bright peering up at her.

"My little helper is clearing the bird's nest," Klaus told

him.

"Like hell she is," Bright muttered. "Mary, please get down."

Mary started back down the ladder, her legs feeling a bit wobbly. Her foot slipped a little and she let out a little squeal. Another hand came up to steady her, resting pretty close to her bottom. "That's it. You're okay. Two more," he said. The heat of his hand seared through her dress and her heart beat faster, but she wasn't sure now that it was from fear.

"Thank you," she said when she got to the ground, her cheeks flushed.

He took his hand away from where it was resting, very near her butt cheek.

"Sorry," he muttered.

"What about the nest?" his dad asked.

"I'll call maintenance," Mary told him.

"No, no, they won't get here for ages, it needs clearing." Klaus was getting rather agitated, his cheeks rosy.

"Dad, calm down," Bright said. "It's not urgent."

"It is urgent!" Klaus shouted.

"Okay, fine, I'll get it," Bright said. "Would you mind holding the ladder?" he asked Mary.

She tried not to watch his thighs and bottom as he ascended, but it was hard. She was right there after all and she needed to look up to hold onto the ladder and do her job, surely.

He was quickly back down, faster than she could have

managed, carrying a small nest. In it were two chicks, beaks open, squawking for their mother. A robin started to chirp loudly from a nearby tōtara tree.

"All right, mama," Bright called. "Relax."

More gently than Mary would have thought him capable, he carried the baby birds over to the tree and reached up to place the nest in the V of a branch. He stepped back and they all watched as the mother bird circled nervously around until she eventually plucked up the courage to go near the nest, chirping away the whole time.

"She's letting me know what's what," Klaus said, somewhat cryptically. Bright gave his dad a gentle pat on the shoulder.

"How about we take this ladder back to where you found it then?"

Mary watched as he led his dad away, his face inscrutable. She tried not to think about his hand on her bottom and how nice it had felt.

CHAPTER 8

Hanging up lights causes the most Christmas-related injuries every year and three people die annually from testing with their tongue if a nine-volt battery works.

Bright

There was something wrong with the electric blinds in Andrew's office. They kept raising and lowering themselves at will. The glare on Bright's computer screen was awful so he packed up his laptop and headed into the clubhouse to try to find somewhere to get some work done.

He was also avoiding Dougal who seemed to have a tireless supply of comments and complaints to be made. It was a mere coincidence that he ended up in the library where he could see Mary working away at her own laptop. After all, that was what the internet zone was used for, he told himself.

One of the lamps in the corner kept flickering on and off like some sort of Morse code, so he got up and unplugged it. What on earth was up with all the electrics here? From where he stood, he could see Mary making notes. She had reindeer earrings on today, the noses little glowing red lights. Every now and then she paused to think, tapping her pen against the notepad in time to the radio. He wondered what she was thinking about. When she looked up and noticed him staring, she gave him a warm smile.

"Someone's been pinching my socks," Dougal said in his ear, making him jump. It would seem he hadn't gone far enough from his office. "This is the third one to go missing."

"You've lost three pairs of socks?" Bright clarified.

"No, no, just the one."

"One pair?"

"No." Dougal sighed loudly. "Three socks. One sock each time, not a pair. From my clothesline."

"Are you sure your washing machine isn't eating them?" Mary called out helpfully.

"Yes, I'm sure. I'm not a flaming idiot, I know I hung both socks out each time. And three times, one of them has disappeared. Someone is nicking them," Dougal huffed.

"Why would anyone want only one sock?" Mary asked.

"How the hell should I know?" Dougal grumbled. "Maybe it's that bloke up at forty-three with the prosthetic leg?"

"Ohhh," Mary said. "Yes, Marvin Petrois. That's a fair assessment. No, wait. I think he's gone to the hospital and doesn't get around much these days."

"Well, he managed fine before with one leg, didn't he?" Dougal grumbled.

Bright sighed. "I'm really not sure that there's much to be done about three missing socks to be honest, Mr Cartwright."

"Four," Bets called out from the hallway.

"Sorry?" Bright could feel the start of a headache forming. He really needed a coffee.

"I couldn't help but overhear," Bets said. "I lost one of my lovely green bed socks last week."

"Right," Bright said, rubbing his forehead. "Well, I'll make a note ..."

"And Helen and Viv have both lost a knee-high."

"A what?"

"Knee-high. Stockings, love. I only remember this because they were saying how odd it was that they lost one each. And how it was a shame they didn't match as they could have paired up the other two if they did. But one was a thick navy and the other was a spotty one. A compression one, I believe, you know, for on the aeroplane. Stops you getting an STD ..."

"I think you'll find it's DVT," Mary said with a sort of laughing cough. Bright held back a grin.

"I'll look into it then."

"The case of the missing socks," Bets said, clapping her hands together. "How exciting."

"Riveting," said Mary with such a straight face that he had to look up and catch her wink to realise she was being sarcastic.

"Perhaps, Ms Star," he said, "we could have a meeting over a coffee and discuss our sleuthing technique?"

"Excellent idea, Bright," she said, and there was something rather nice about the way she said his name. He thought perhaps he liked it.

The cafe at the clubhouse was fairly small. It had a long servery area with a glass cabinet of various cakes and slices and also a pie warmer with sausage rolls and mini quiches. A robust woman stood behind the counter taking drink orders, her hair in a net, a smudge of orange lipstick on one tooth.

"What can I get you?" Bright asked Mary.

"I'd love a flat white, thanks. Shall I get us a water each and nab a table?"

Bright ordered their hot drinks and then eyed the cakes. He didn't have much of a sweet tooth but he'd noticed Mary did. He ordered a couple of brandy snaps as well and paid.

Mary had picked a table at the back by the ranch sliders and she was sitting watching him, a smile on her face. He smiled back but then stopped. Glenda had stopped to chat to her, along with a young guy in a garishly bright tie-dyed T-shirt. Bright didn't like the way he had his hand on Mary's shoulder. There was something a little too familiar about it.

"Here he is," Mary said. "Dallas, this is Bright, our temporary manager. Bright, this is Dallas, Glenda's grandson, visiting from Dunedin."

"Hey, mate." Dallas gave him a head nod. Bright put out his hand, forcing Dallas to remove his from Mary and shake it.

"I was telling Mary that she should join Dallas for dinner tonight," Glenda told him. "I booked us a table at La Dolce but silly old me forgot that I have bridge."

"That really is kind, but I'm afraid I already have plans," Mary said, and for some reason Bright felt quite relieved. He briefly wondered what her plans might be.

Bright thought that they'd never leave. Dallas was hovering around Mary like a skunk to a sunflower and Glenda continued to natter away. He watched Mary, listening to Glenda, her head tilted to one side, silly earrings swaying each time she nodded, like she genuinely was interested in what Glenda had to say.

"Well, I'd best get back and get my washing in. Last week I had one of my lucky lawn bowls socks go missing. There were dirty boot marks on the pavers too, so I don't think it fell off and blew away. Why on earth would anybody want a single sock?"

"It is a bit strange," Mary said.

"I'm a bit worried they might come back for my ..." She leant in to whisper furtively to Mary, but not quietly enough that Bright couldn't hear. "... smalls."

"Right. Let's hope not. I understand you wanting to hurry off though."

"Panty thieves, they're called. It's disgusting to think what they might be doing with them." Glenda shuddered dramatically.

"It was nice to see you again, Dallas," Mary said, when Glenda turned to leave, gesturing for him to follow.

"You'll be seeing a bit more of me, no doubt. I'm here for a while scouting out jobs."

Bright gritted his teeth and hoped the job market wasn't favourable. There was nothing small about Glenda, he thought, as her ample backside made its way between tables towards the exit. He couldn't think of one single thing a pair of granny pants would be useful for — other than polishing the car, maybe.

Mary's eyes sparkled, as though she could tell what he was thinking.

"Gran would have called them her apple catchers," she said with a grin as she took a sip of her coffee, then picked up the brandy snap and took a large bite, moaning apprecia- tively. "Mmm, delicious. These are one of my favourite treats at Christmas."

There was a blob of cream on her lip and Bright thought about reaching out and rubbing it off with his finger, but Mary picked up her serviette and dabbed her lips and he mentally shook himself for such an idiotic idea.

He felt oddly tongue-tied and drank his coffee way too

fast, burning his tongue. They finished much quicker than he would have liked.

"So the socks?" Mary asked with a grin.

"Yes, I doubt it's anything more than forgetfulness, but I suppose I can sort something out. See if there's anything to worry about."

"Well, let me know if there's anything you want me to help with. Thanks for the coffee, Bright. I'm sure you've got loads to do, so I'll head off and see Mrs Greene at number thirty-two." Mary stood and hoisted up the overstuffed tote bag she lugged around with her. "She hasn't been well. I've made some soup and I want to see if there's anything she needs."

"I'll get on to the security stuff," he said. He had a friend in the business who owed him a favour. Mary weaved through the tables, smiling and waving at the residents. As he followed behind her, he couldn't help but think about underwear. Not the type Glenda would be wearing either.

THE NEWSIE

Anyone needing a lift down to Clip and Shave for a haircut, please let Mary know by 8 am.

Congratulations and happy 60th wedding anniversary to Bob and Lindy Peterson.

Anyone interested in learning about Skype and FaceTime, Janice is holding a workshop in the rec room at 1.30 pm.

CHAPTER 9

Mary

Ada Greene, one of their most senior residents, was feeling a bit perkier after the doctor's visit earlier that morning and Mary was pleased. Ada had been looking very frail lately and had seemed more tired than usual since her one hundredth birthday the month before. Mary heated up the soup and had a chat about the possibility of Ada moving into a room in the local rest home. Another resident had recently transferred out of town to be closer to her family and Mary, who was friendly with the manager, knew the available room had a lovely view of the garden and morning sun. Ada had been reluctant in the past to give up her independence. "I've managed on my own for almost fifty years. That's half a century," she said, as she always did. But she agreed to go with Mary to have a look when she was feeling better. Ada gave her a small list of things she needed and Mary offered to pick up her prescription from the chemist. It was near the barber's and she was due to take Klaus for his monthly trim and beard tidy that afternoon.

Mary popped in to see Jerry on her way back to the main building to pick up the van. He was sitting on his front step polishing his brown brogues.

"I'm taking Klaus out for a haircut," she called. "Thought maybe you might like to join us?"

"I went last week," he said. "Are you saying I'm looking a bit scruffy?" His eyes twinkled.

"I'd never call you scruffy, Jerry. You're one of the most dapper men in the village."

"Anyway, I'm off to see Lois. She's been having some kind of trouble with her Christmas tree lights and asked me to take a look. Not that I'm an electrician or anything, but I'll see what I can do."

"That's kind of you." Mary hadn't noticed anything wrong with Lois's lights when she'd been there earlier in the week.

"Well, she's a lovely lady, always looking out for me. There will probably be a cup of tea and some baking for my efforts." He pulled himself up slowly and brushed off his trousers. "I think she misses her wee grandchildren a lot. We've got to look out for each other, us oldies." He picked up his toolbox and Mary gave him a wave and headed across the lawn to the clubhouse.

There was hammering coming from inside the garage when she arrived at Klaus's house. Mary rang the bell several times and was about to head around the back when he finally opened the front door.

"Mary. What a nice surprise." Klaus tucked a set of keys into his pocket.

"I'm here to take you to the barber. I thought we could stop somewhere and get afternoon tea afterwards."

"The barber?"

"Yes, you were going to write it on your calendar."

"I don't need to go to the barber."

Mary eyed his hair which had started to curl onto his collar, and his beard which was definitely getting woolly. Klaus was usually so pedantic about this.

"We could go next week if you'd rather?"

"I told you I don't need a haircut," Klaus said belligerently. "I wouldn't mind going for afternoon tea though. Could we get some of those mince tarts?"

"Of course," she agreed. "As long as you don't mind tagging along on some errands I need to run. Shall we have a look and see if there's anything you need at the supermarket?"

Klaus led the way into the kitchen. He smelt of sawdust and furniture oil. For some reason it made her think of Bright's sandalwood aftershave.

While Klaus looked to see if he needed any groceries, Mary eyed his calendar. It was one she'd made for him earlier in the year to make it easier to remember dates and events.

There was nothing there about the barber's visit but he definitely had some strange entries. 'Bird whistles' was yesterday. 'Check the list again', 'Buy more wrapping paper' and 'Make a map' were yet to do, apparently.

"I'd like to stop and get some pyjamas, if you don't mind. Mine are all getting too small."

She dropped Klaus at home with the two extra mince tarts he'd insisted he was saving 'for later' and then called in to Ada with her antibiotics and groceries before returning the van to the main building. There was a yellow work truck with an outline of an eye and 'Eye Spy Security' in black parked in the front car park. Two men in company polo shirts were loading equipment back into the car. Bright had got onto that quickly, she thought. Unusually so, considering he didn't seem to like spending money unnecessarily. Could it be the thought of having to field complaints about missing underwear from the residents that had spurred him into action?

The decorations from previous Christmases were stored in large plastic tubs in the rec room storage cupboards. Mary decided to pull them out and sort through what they had. Bright came in as she was detangling the third set of lights, which she could have sworn she'd looped so carefully the year before.

"I took your dad out," she told him, plugging the lights in to check they were working. They were. No need to get Jerry in to save the day. "We were meant to be going to the barber but he refused. He's usually so particular about having his hair and beard tidied."

"That doesn't sound like him." The furrow she was becoming used to seeing appeared in his brow again. "What with losing the keys to the garage and being secretive. I'm wondering whether he's taken a bit of a downward turn."

"Well, he must have found the keys. He was in the garage when I called in and was putting them into his pocket. The car was still outside though."

"I'll call in when I've finished here and put it away for him."

"You probably will notice things about your dad that are different from before," Mary said gently. She thought of the strange list of things on the calendar. "Independence is so important and it's normal to resist help, especially at this stage. But he has a lot of love and support here."

"I'm starting to see that."

"And he's lucky to have you. You obviously have a very close relationship. That can make it hard, when he's not the dad you used to know."

Bright blinked and stared out the window, his frown deepening. "I appreciate everything you do," he said gruffly.

"Oh, it's a pleasure. He's still a gentleman, your dad." Mary laughed. "Still insisted on paying for afternoon tea for us both. Though why he thought we needed six mince tarts between us, I've no idea."

"Bloody hell, the greedy bugger. He definitely doesn't need that." Bright gave a little chuckle and Mary noticed the way his eyes crinkled.

"Do you mind if I take the van tomorrow to pick up a Christmas tree?" she asked. "I usually go and get a nice one from a tree farm out of town. It's the only place that grows them big enough to fill the living area."

"Sure. I imagine you're the only one who uses it anyway."

Mary thought she'd strike while he seemed to be in a good mood. "It's a bit of a mission, getting it into the van by myself. I don't suppose you could come with me and give me a hand? If you're not too busy."

Bright eyed her up and down dubiously, as though taking in her small stature and imagining her single-handedly hauling a hulking pine tree on her shoulder.

"I could do that. I've got to check on my other business in the morning and then I have a few things to sort here, so maybe around eleven?"

"Thanks, Bright, I'd appreciate that."

Although Tony, the owner of the Christmas tree farm, wouldn't, she thought. He prided himself on helping everyone to get their trees into cars and trailers and securely and safely tied down for the trip home.

CHAPTER 10

*Shirley Temple stopped believing in Santa at six, when
her mother took her to see him at the mall and he asked
for her autograph.*

Bright

"They're lost, I tell you. I haven't got them."

"Mary seemed to think you had them this afternoon," Bright said, rummaging through Klaus's wardrobe checking his dad's pockets for keys.

"She's imagining it," Klaus said firmly.

"Well, then where were you when I knocked? It sounded like you came from the garage."

"What garage?"

"Yours, Dad."

"Can't have. It's locked."

"Why on earth have you got so many pairs of red pyjamas?" Bright asked. "You don't even like red."

"They were on sale. Now get out of my drawers."

Bright sighed and headed back down the hallway to check the garage door again. It was still locked but there was a definite trail of something along the carpet. He bent down and picked some of it up between his fingers. It was grainy and smelt like fresh wood chips.

"Dad, what's going on? You've clearly been in the garage, so you must know where the key is. What's in there you don't want me to see?"

Klaus gave him a funny look. "Your mother loves Christmas," he said. "Mad about it."

"Yes, Dad, she did." Bright was unsure if he should mention to his dad how long she had been gone.

"You boys always wanted a toy garage," Klaus added. "What day is it? Is it Friday?"

Bright sighed. "How about I make us some dinner," he said. "Steak maybe? And some salad?"

"Chips and eggs would be better," Klaus said, giving Bright a beaming smile. "You're a good boy."

The next morning Bright arrived at the Palms feeling a bit awkward. He'd been into Dainty Dwellings earlier and Gary had been shocked to see him out of 'uniform' and it had made him self-conscious. He normally wore suit pants and a shirt to work, but he'd thought it might be a bit silly to wear them to cut down a tree so he'd put on a pair of jeans and a pale-pink collared polo instead. Now, he was stupidly worried about what Mary might think of his clothes. Was it too casual?

When she arrived, she had on a pair of yellow shorts and a T-shirt with Snoopy in a Santa hat on the front. Today's earrings were candy canes. She should have looked like a twelve year old. Should have, but didn't.

"That pink is lovely on you," she said, and he stopped worrying about what he was wearing.

"I have the van ready." He gestured to where it was parked around the side of the offices. "I took it to get gassed up. I wasn't sure how far we were going."

"Have you never been to Tony's Tree Farm? I thought everyone went there for trees," Mary said, climbing into the passenger seat. Bright resisted the urge to help, trying not to think of the feeling of her bottom in his hand. He adjusted himself and got in behind the wheel.

"Tell me you're not a fake-tree person?" She held her hand theatrically over her heart.

"Dad and I don't get a tree," he said, pulling away from the kerb. "Haven't done for years. Not since Mum was here. She died right before Christmas."

"That's so sad. I'm so sorry. No wonder you're not that keen on Christmas." Mary put on her belt.

"Dad never wanted to celebrate after she died. She was a big fan of Christmas, went all out celebrating it, and I think it reminded him too much of what he'd lost." He felt a bit embarrassed, telling her that. He wasn't sure why he had.

"What you *all* lost," she said quietly. "Left at the lights here."

"I should have let you drive." He looked quickly over at her and away. There was a lull in conversation for a bit, except for her giving him the occasional direction towards the tree farm.

"What about *your* parents?" he asked, to break the silence.

"Well, I never knew my dad," she said. "And my mother wasn't really able to raise a child. She was an addict and she had mental health issues, so when I was little, I didn't even know what Christmas was. It wasn't until I went to live with my Gran when I was nine that I celebrated my first Christmas Day. Next right."

"I'm really sorry," Bright said. He felt terrible for asking.

"Oh, don't be sorry." Mary gave him a pat on his shoulder as if to comfort him. "Gran made Christmas wonderful. She went all out every year until she died, all the decorations, carols, crafts — the works. She made me love Christmas." She gave him a wink. "You might have realised I'm a bit of a fan. Like your mum."

"I hadn't noticed," Bright said. But they were both grinning.

Tony, a beefy bloke with a buzz cut and a wonky left eye, had turned out to be a pretty good bloke and had insisted on helping Bright load the tree into the van. They'd underestimated the tree's size and the trunk stuck out the back door half a metre, so they'd used some twine and tied the doors as best as possible and hung Bright's white hanky to a lower branch as a warning to any following car. Tony had thrown in a small tree for Mary, free of charge, and a couple of packets of fringe-style tinsel too.

"Shall we drop your tree off at your place first?" Bright suggested.

Mary's house was very *her*. A small cottage set close to the road, pale yellow with a garden bed bursting with colour along the path to her candy-pink door. Inside it was warm and inviting, with a large stuffed couch draped in a crochet rug and a standing lamp that was zebra striped. There was art everywhere, and framed photos of her as a young girl, then a teen and up, her grandmother ageing alongside her.

"Gran left me the house when she died," Mary told him. "This was her bedroom before. I couldn't bring myself to sleep in it, so I turned it into the lounge. The plan is to renovate the old lounge and make the kitchen and dining area bigger, once I get some more money saved."

"I could probably help you with planning and design," Bright told her. "This is practically the size of one of our tiny houses."

"Hmm, maybe." Mary looked away, and he wondered if that had come out a bit like a criticism. Was she offended?

"I didn't mean ..."

"I think this corner could work?" Mary said, moving a round coffee table out of the way to sit in front of the couch. "I'll just get the tree stand."

They set up the tree and admired their work.

"Thanks, Bright," Mary said. "Did you want a cup of tea, or shall we head back and get the tree sorted at the Palms?"

Bright wanted to suggest they sit on her couch and talk a bit more, or something, but it was almost one o'clock and he needed to take his father for a doctor's appointment at two.

"We'd better head back," he said reluctantly. "Sorry."

"Well, if you're not doing anything later, perhaps you'd like to come over for a meal? Or a drink? You could even help me decorate the tree?" Mary gestured to the top. "It's not big, but I still may need help getting anything up on the tip of it."

Bright rather desperately wanted to say yes. So he did.

CHAPTER 11

Tinsel was originally made with real silver.

Bright

Doctor Eastman was almost as old as Klaus and more stooped over. He still wrote his notes by hand and told Bright that his secretary typed them out for him later. His handwriting was stereotypically bad — a chicken scratch that Bright could not decipher and he imagined was a nightmare to transcribe.

"You've put on a fair bit of weight," the doctor told Klaus.

"Good, good," his father said, looking pleased.

"I don't think that was meant to be complimentary, Dad," Bright told him. "You were supposed to be watching what you eat."

"I'll look at a diet in the New Year," Klaus said, holding on to the exam table while he put his shoes back on.

"You're at high risk of developing diabetes," the doctor

said. "And your face is rather rosy. We'd better check your blood pressure."

Klaus sat and waited while the doctor wrapped the cuff around his arm.

"How have you been feeling?" the doctor asked. "Memory any worse?" He looked at Bright when he asked this.

"I'm jolly well fine," Klaus said.

While Bright was settling the bill, he turned around to find Klaus sitting in the waiting room, playing with an abacus alongside a small boy at the play table. He said something to him and the boy broke into a beaming smile.

"Really?" he asked, and Klaus nodded. "I have been," the boy said.

"I know," Klaus told him, tapping the side of his nose.

"Tyler, come on," his mother called. The boy waved furiously at Klaus as he was led into the doctor's consultation room.

"Bye, Santa," he called. Bright laughed. He could see why the boy had thought that, with Klaus's white hair and beard. It really could do with a trim.

"How about we stop and get you a haircut on the way home?" he suggested.

"I'll look at that in the New Year," Klaus said. "But I wouldn't mind an ice cream."

Bright picked up a couple of bottles of wine on the way back to Mary's that evening. He wasn't sure if she was a red or a white drinker, so he got both. The lights were on and he could hear music playing. Through the window, he could see her dancing around in the kitchen, a wooden spoon up to her mouth in what he suspected might be a pretend microphone.

She wasn't his type. He normally chose more sedate, career-focused women. Not that he'd had a girlfriend for a while. It had been ... bloody hell ... longer than he'd realised. His last girlfriend, Greta, had been well over a year ago. She had been in corporate law. Things had been fine with them, but it had fizzled out after about eighteen months when she had talked about him moving in with her. He wasn't attached to his townhouse particularly, but he wasn't attached to her apartment either. He'd imagined they might get a house together, maybe a dog. Possibly even have a kid, although he wasn't fussed either way on that. But Greta had looked at him like he'd suggested they become nudists and he'd realised they had never talked about the future together.

Mary was nothing like Greta. Or Lisa the accountant, or Hayley the accountant, or, bloody hell, Kelly — who was also an accountant. What was that all about?

They'd all been tall and well ... sensible looking was what came to mind. Tidy haircuts and those suits with skirts and small heels. Not pink hair and mad earrings and T-shirts with cartoons.

But Mary did remind him of someone. His mother, he realised with a jolt. Not the hair and clothes, but her enthusiasm for life. The way she found joy in little things. How easily she laughed. And her kindness. He wondered if she was seeing anyone? Would she have invited him around if she was? What sort of men did she go for? Probably not ones like him. He was too serious. Too boring probably.

She wasn't his type, but he realised he wanted to be hers.

The house smelt of lemon and pine needles when Mary answered the door and gestured him in. She was wearing elf slippers, he noted with amusement. They had pointy toes with little bells on the end. There were boxes of decorations and lights scattered around the tree and Count Basie was playing on the stereo. He handed her the wine and she gave him a beaming smile.

"Will I open one for you? I have a Pinot Gris open already but it's likely not as good."

"Whatever you have will be fine," he said. "Thank you."

She went into the kitchen and he heard her rummaging around, opening the fridge and a cupboard, glasses clinking.

"I've made a risotto. I wasn't sure if you had any food allergies, or if you ate meat ..." She came back in, carrying a wine for him and handed it over.

"It smells lovely. And I eat almost anything. Except almond icing."

"Good to know." She gestured to the couch. "Shall we sit?

Or would you prefer to eat now?"

"Let's sit if that's okay? I had an ice cream with Dad earlier, so I'm not starving." He took a sip of wine. "I feel a bit guilty. He's supposed to be looking after his weight, but he insisted. I should have said no."

"Ah well, Gran always said 'Life happens right now, not tomorrow' and I tend to think she was right. I see all these elderly people who have regrets, some for what they did do, and some for what they didn't, and I think either way, you have to live for the moment, make your own happiness, you know? Eat the ice cream while you can."

She had lovely lips. Wide and plump and kissable. Bright found himself staring at them too long as she talked. He looked around for a distraction.

"Are all these boxes for the tree?" he asked.

"Well, let's see. The tree's probably too small and it'll keel over with the weight of them, but they all have meaning and I love seeing them hanging on the branches." She took a gulp of wine and put her glass down on the table. "I was sort of hoping I could rope you into doing the lights? With you being so tall, I won't have to get out the step ladder."

"How short are you anyway?" Bright asked and she laughed.

"I'm a perfectly respectable height, thank you very much. You're just over-tall."

Bright grinned and got up to help string the lights.

"I'm not that tall," he said. "My brother tells everyone he's an inch taller than he is, but I'm sure he's the same height as me. How do you want these?"

They stopped to eat, opened Bright's bottle of riesling, and gradually hung the bulk of the decorations, with Mary telling him about which ones she had picked with her gran and others she had picked up on her travels. She'd seen a lot of the world, mostly backpacking. He had done only a few trips with Bern in his twenties and the odd conference to the States. He was envious of her spirit of adventure.

"I did a bit of travel in my twenties and after Gran passed as well." Mary untangled the string from a glass bauble with a snowflake suspended inside it. "She was a good budgeter and a saver so I inherited her life savings, as well as this house. She never went far from home but always loved hearing stories of my trips. Especially England, where her mother was from."

"What did you do there?"

"All sorts. I travelled around and did a bit of bar work, cleaning, that sort of thing. My boyfriend at the time was a plumber. He ended up finding a permanent job and staying on."

She passed the untangled bauble to Bright. "I think this would look nice near the top over there. I brought that one back from Switzerland, because Gran loved the snow but she'd never seen it. Carried it in my hand luggage all the way home." Mary stopped and put her hands on her hips, observing the tree. Bright wanted to pick her up and put her on the top.

"Gran got sick and before she died she told me to make the most of life. I try to do that every day."

The daily grind was how Bright thought of his life. Work, business commitments, trying to figure out how he could make more money. No time for fun.

"Now just some of these tinsel strands and we're done." Mary hung a Mickey Mouse figure on a lower branch.

"You're lucky you don't have a cat," Bright noted.

"Oh, but I'd love one. Gran had a big tom called Purrbury when I first moved in and I adored him." Mary went to top up his glass, but he stopped her.

"Better not, I'm driving. Any reason you haven't got one since?" Mary filled her own glass, finishing the bottle.

"I was travelling too much initially, and then my ex was allergic, but now ... I'm waiting for the cat to find me."

"Huh? How does that work?"

"Oh, you know, animals have a way of coming into your life and then they're meant to be. Purrbury was a stray and he just turned up and owned us." Mary unwrapped an angel from some tissue paper. "Would you like to do the honours? I can't reach."

"Why don't I give you a lift," he said with a laugh, picking her up by the hips and lifting her easily up to place the decoration on top of the tree. She squealed and they both laughed while she popped it on and then he slowly lowered her down, wishing he had a reason to keep holding on to her.

There was a bit of an uncomfortable silence as they stood looking at each other and then he cleared his throat and Mary went over to the wall, bending down to turn on the switch. He tried not to look at her bum. It was getting a bit ridiculous how often he had to stop himself.

"Ready? Voilà!" The lights glowed on the tree, catching the silver tinsel strands and reflecting like stars. Bright had forgotten how nice it was seeing the end result of dressing a Christmas tree. He thought again of his mother and how she would let him and Bern put on the decorations in any haphazard way they chose, insisting it was the best tree they'd ever had, year after year. How his dad would lift one of them up to put the star at the top and then the other to 'reput it'. A lump formed in his throat.

"I'd better get going," he said, a little brusquely. "Thanks for dinner."

"No, thank you," Mary said gently, and then he left, driving home feeling like an idiot for crying in the dark of his car.

THE NEWSIE

Happy hour drinks special tonight Midori and lemonade for just $3!

Natty Knitters group will now meet in the lounge, not the library, at 10 am due to some lighting issues.

Sorry to those who found the pool too cold yesterday, there was a fault with the heat pump.

CHAPTER 12

Mary

Jerry was out watering his garden when Mary went past the next morning.

"Your roses are looking beautiful," she called to him. "What are they called?"

"Lovely Lady," he told her. "They're smashing, aren't they? Almost match your hair." He gave one a gentle stroke. "I grew them for my late wife. Picked her a bunch every anniversary to tell her I loved her." He gave Mary a sad smile. "Where are you off to so early?"

"I thought I'd get in some laps at the pool before I start the day. What about you? What are your plans?"

"I'm going to pop over to Glenda's after breakfast. She has a bathroom cabinet that's squeaking a bit, needs a bit of oiling, I think."

"You know maintenance can do that? I'm happy to call them?"

"No, no. It's no bother. I fixed Lois's kitchen hinges yesterday, took me five minutes. I'm happy to do it. Besides, it's the least I can do when Lois irons all my shirts for me." He gave her a conspiratorial wink. "I might get a piece of Glenda's famous baking if I time it right."

Mary laughed. "You might have them duelling at dawn if you're not careful, Jerry."

He looked a little baffled. "Pardon me? Goodness, you don't think Glenda thinks ...? Cripes. I hadn't thought ..."

Mary laughed. "You're a bit of a catch, Jerry. There are not many single men in the village, and none as well dressed as you."

"And all my own teeth," Jerry said, pretending to bite her. "No, I'm sure you're imagining things. Now go have your swim." He gave the hose a flick in her direction and she giggled, jumping back.

"See you later," she called, heading over to the pool.

Mary didn't learn to swim until she was almost eleven. She'd been too embarrassed to admit she didn't know how but her gran had realised and insisted she learn. 'We live on an island, surrounded by water,' she'd told Mary. 'And there's nothing better for the mind than swimming.'

She was right. Swimming was Mary's time to stop thinking and just breathe. She loved the peacefulness of being underwater, her focus only on getting to the end of the pool and then back again. Having access to the Palms pool was a great perk of the job.

She put the bag with her clothes and towel on one of the loungers, and went over to the pool edge, pulling her goggles over her eyes.

"Bloody hell," she spluttered as she emerged from her dive in. The pool was normally overly heated for the seniors, but this morning it was stone cold. Mary had gotten used to the pleasant warmth and the cold was jarring.

She did a fast ten laps and then hopped out, shivering. Through the window into the office she could see Bright hunched over his computer, so she wrapped her towel around herself and headed inside through the side door.

"Morning," she called. "I just thought I'd let you know the pool is freezing cold. I'll put a notice on the door but could you get someone to have a look at it?" Mary's hair was dripping unpleasantly cold rivulets down her back so she took her towel off and gave it a vigorous rub. When she looked up, Bright was staring at her and she wished she was wearing something sexier than her practical blue Speedo.

He cleared his throat. "Um ... I was just checking the security footage. Have a look at this."

Mary hovered behind him over the computer, hoping she wasn't going to drip.

"See here?" He pointed at a grainy black and white image. "I had a security team set up a few cameras. This one was placed where you can see Fran Gardener and Bets Jackson's clotheslines in the same shot."

A man in a floppy pointed hat with a pompom on the end was reaching up to remove a sock from Bets' clothesline. Bright flicked to the next image which showed the man, head bent, walking away.

"Unfortunately, there are no clear shots of the culprit's face."

"Is that a Santa hat?" Mary asked, leaning closer. A drop of water fell from her hair onto Bright's arm. It rested there, between two blondish hairs, accentuating the tan of his skin. She took a quick step back, annoyed at how her heart had started beating faster and worried he might somehow be able to hear it.

Bright stared down at the drop of water for a second, then cleared his throat again. He reached up to enlarge the image and the drop slipped slowly down his arm.

"It looks like it could be." He leaned closer to the screen. "It's someone feeling festive then. Do you think they're a resident here?"

"I think they must be." Mary refrained from leaning in for a better look. "The way they're kind of stooped? Looks like an elderly person to me."

"I guess we'll have to see if they come back. I'm puzzled though. What would you do with a bunch of odd socks?"

"Hello, love." Helen put her head around her office door a little later, as Mary was sorting out the events schedule for the following week. "Viv and I would like to put our names down for the shopping trip tomorrow if it's not too late."

Mary had completely forgotten about the shopping trip. She'd planned the craft-making session for the afternoon and had promised Ada she'd call in again too.

"I'll add you both to the list," she said smiling brightly. "We'll try to head off around nine, if everyone is ready."

"There's always someone who's not," Helen said. "You need to say nine sharp, rather than 'around nine', then there's no excuse if they get left behind."

Mary sighed. Helen was right. Sometimes it was impossible to please everyone.

"I'm heading to the media room and I was wondering if you had any new magazines? The ones in there have been there for weeks," Helen said.

"I'll bring some right over."

There was a box in the library where the residents donated magazines they'd read and Mary had noticed there was a good pile, so she abandoned her planning for now.

The Natty Knitters were set up in a corner of the lounge. Dougal was hunched in front of the TV on the opposite side watching the cricket.

"Keep it down over there," he bellowed. "I can hardly hear the commentary over the sound of those bloody needles."

"Thanks for the magazines, love." Helen bent to reel in a

ball of blue wool that had unravelled under her seat. "Have you done all your Christmas shopping?"

Mary wished she had more Christmas shopping to do. Apart from Patsy, she didn't really have friends who exchanged gifts. The Christmas cards had been sent last week and the coconut ice for the residents was already done. She envied people with large families and wrapping-paper-strewn living rooms on Christmas Day.

"Pretty much finished," she said, smiling at Helen. "Are you planning on finishing yours tomorrow on the shopping trip?"

"I've just got to get something for my brother and sister-in-law and something for Viv. That'll be tricky if she's on the trip, won't it? I'll have to get someone to distract her, I think."

"Will we be able to call in to the hardware store on the way back?" Bets asked. She was sitting beside Helen, knitting something grey and speckled. "There isn't one at the mall."

"That should be fine." She might have to move the craft session to later.

A buzzing noise and then a loud *pop* made them all jump. The TV screen flickered twice and then went blank.

"What's happened to the bloody cricket?" Dougal threw his hands up.

Helen got up to investigate. "If you just ..."

There was a flash, the screen blinked again and the TV came back on.

"For crying out loud, that's not the Black Caps."

There was a smiling woman with a neat bob and pink lipstick, holding aloft a purple drink bottle that had a strange screwtop attached. "… and with every bottle and set of three Flavour Infusion Pods, we'll throw in an extra pack of limited edition cranberry flavour."

"That's perfect." Helen put one hand over her heart. "I've been telling Viv she needs to hydrate while she's out walking, but she's not all that keen on the taste of water. This would be the perfect present. Quick, Dougal, write the number down."

"I was watching the bloody cricket," Dougal grumbled to nobody in particular.

"Mary, do you have a pen, love?" Helen asked.

"I'll take a screenshot for you." Mary took out her phone and took a photo just as Dougal realised he was sitting on the remote control.

He changed channels and the cricket came back on. "I've missed the beginning of the next innings now."

"You were the one sitting on the remote," Helen retorted, but she was looking very pleased.

CHAPTER 13

It is a tradition in Japan to eat KFC for Christmas.
Orders must be placed two months in advance.

Bright

There was another pile of parcels from AliExpress, all addressed to Klaus. Bright took them down to his dad's, peering around the stack and then struggling to balance them all as he tried to get in the front door. Klaus wasn't answering and there was no sign of him inside.

The house smelt strongly of fried food, so he stacked the packages on the bench and went to the sliding doors, opening them wide to let in some fresh air. Klaus's neighbours, Dale and Sherry, were outside at their patio table with a large jug of something fruity and not nearly enough clothing, if you asked Bright. Sherry was in some sort of minimalist crochet bikini, while Dale had on a pair of canary-yellow speedos.

"Why, hello there, Bright," Sherry called, jiggling the ice cubes in the jug as she poured a drink, her own jugs also swaying in a most alarming way. "Fancy a Pimm's?"

"Thanks, but no," Bright said, looking intently over Sherry's shoulder at her bird bath. "Have you seen Dad at all?"

"He was over earlier, asking to borrow a belt," Dale told him, standing up and coming closer to Bright, belly preceding him. "He needed something with a bit more girth, and I've definitely got that." He gave his ample belly a rub.

"You most certainly have, darling," Sherry said, stretching out one leg and giving her husband's bottom a poke with a manicured toe, winking at Bright.

"Right, well." Bright cleared his throat. "I'll leave you to enjoy the sun then."

"Right you are," Dale said. "Feel free to join us any time."

There was a large bucket of fried chicken in the fridge, along with two chocolate mousse containers. On the bench was a Christmas cake with a large wedge missing from it. Bright was looking in the pantry to see what else his father was eating when the TV suddenly flicked on.

A low-pixel image of his mother, dressed in a nightgown, holding a plate and smiling at the camera, was frozen on the screen. Behind her was a Christmas tree and the old mustard-yellow couch Bright remembered from their family home. He stood and stared at the screen for a few minutes, taking in his mother's face. When he finally moved closer, he realised his dad had been watching home movies, with the old VCR hooked up to the back of the TV. He hit play, then watched as his mother put down the plate of cookies on the wooden coffee table and beckoned to someone. A man in a Santa suit came into view and the pair hugged, then slow danced in the lounge, his mother laughing and then his father's face coming into view. Klaus looked so young, his eyes twinkling, and he kissed his wife, lifting her up as he did, hands under her bottom.

Bright could remember the night Santa had visited them. It was Christmas Eve and he and Bern had been squeezing the gifts under the tree, hoping to figure out what they could be, when there was a knock at the door. Santa had come in, sat on their couch and asked them in a gruff voice what they wanted for Christmas.

"Ask them if they've been good enough," his mother had said with a laugh, taking a photo of the three of them.

Of course, they must at some point have realised it was their father, years later, Bright assumed, but he didn't recall when. He and Bern had been awestruck to see Santa.

Had his mother known then that she was sick? he wondered. He turned off the video. Why was Klaus watching it now? And where the hell was he?

Bright tried the garage door again. Still locked. He made a mental note to call a locksmith.

On his way back to the office, he passed Dallas, leaning against the outside wall of the entryway, talking to someone on the phone.

"Well, I can only imagine how hot you looked in that, babe," he was saying. "Unless you send me a picture? Something to keep me warm in bed later?" He gave Bright a head nod as he passed. "Nah, babe, you know you're the only girl for me. I haven't even noticed ..."

Bright gave him a friendly smile as he went past. He seemed a good bloke really, he thought. He might have been a bit quick to judge the first time they met.

He went looking for Mary. They needed to go over some Christmas things, and perhaps they could do it over lunch? Jerry was in the foyer, a peaked cap on his head, jangling a set of keys.

"Off for a drive?" Bright asked him.

"Yes, popping down to the garden centre. I need some snail bait and a bit of mulch. I was going to ask if anyone else needed anything." They headed into the clubhouse, both looking around. Mary was at a table, a pile of crepe paper, scissors and tape around her, making paper chains with Lois and Glenda.

"Would anyone like me to pick them up any gardening supplies while I'm out?" Jerry asked.

"Are you going now?" Glenda asked, smoothing her hair.

"I wouldn't mind coming for a drive to keep you company?"

"Oh, well, I mean, right ... yes, of course ..."

Bright thought Jerry looked a little concerned. "Lois, perhaps you'd like to join us?"

Lois looked pleased. Glenda less so.

"That would be lovely, Jerry. Mary, you don't mind if we leave the rest to you, do you?"

"No, no, that's fine," Mary said. "I can finish these off tonight if need be." She looked a little tired, Bright thought, her smile a little strained.

"Perhaps I could help?" he found himself saying. Mary looked at him in surprise. "While we go over the menu for the Christmas party?" he added.

"Oh, lovely, I do hope we're having a nice hot ham?" Glenda said.

"I much prefer turkey myself," Lois said.

"We never had turkey when I was a girl," Glenda said. "Ham is really more traditional."

"Well, you should never be too old to move with the times," Lois was saying as they headed out, Jerry looking back and forward between them, a bewildered look on his face.

"So, what do I do?" Bright asked, waving a hand over the table and the decorating supplies scattered there.

"I'll show you." Mary passed him a pair of scissors. "Thank you."

"You may not say that when I tell you I've had to cut the budget for the lunch," he said.

THE NEWSIE

A reminder that the monthly Palms meeting will be held tomorrow in the lounge at 2 pm. Please see Viv Saunders if there are any items you'd like added to the agenda.

Sherry and Dale will be holding a slide evening of their recent cruise to Hawaii, next Thursday, 5 pm at number 63. Bring a bottle, if you'd like — snacks provided. All welcome.

Has anyone lost a rose gold and white hearing aid? Please see Janice in the office.

There will be a box in the rec room for the Charity Toy Drive. New, wrapped, unisex items only and please indicate a suitable age range on the label. No toy guns, please.

CHAPTER 14

Mary

Mary was laying out pool noodles for the aqua aerobics class when Glenda came in with Dallas.

"I'm going to get my togs on, thanks for walking me over, love," Glenda said as she headed for the changing rooms.

Dallas wandered over and gave Mary a grin. He had a nice, friendly smile and an easy way about him. "Nan said you're organising the Christmas party for the oldies."

"That's right. But some of them might take offence at being called oldies," Mary laughed. "I prefer sen-agers."

"As in senile?" Dallas flashed another smile.

"No, silly." She hit him lightly on the arm. "Seniors. Have some respect for those 'oldies'. You'll be there one day yourself, if you're lucky."

The door opened and Lois walked in with Viv and Helen. "Morning, Mary, we're ready for our workout. Have you got some jazzy music for us today?"

"I'm on to it, Lois." She bent to fiddle with the CD player. "This thing is on its last legs. I'll have to use my phone for the Christmas party at this rate."

"That's actually what I wanted to talk to you about," Dallas said. "Did Nan tell you I do a bit of deejaying in my spare time?" He leant over and took the CD player from Mary to have a closer look. "This thing is shit. You'll never get a decent sound from it."

"As long as we've got music, I don't think it matters too much what it sounds like." Mary took the device back from him and fiddled with the buttons. "Though it kept stopping during the lesson last week."

"Well, I'm here to offer my services." He opened his arms wide and gave Mary another grin. "Whatever those services may be."

The ladies, now joined by Sherry and Bets, had emerged from the changing rooms. "Are we getting started then?" Lois asked. "I don't want to take my towel off if there are strange men present."

"That's my grandson Dallas," Glenda huffed. "He's not strange."

"I could be strange." Dallas winked at Mary. "Depends on what you're into, I guess."

"We're into getting our class started on time, young man," Lois said firmly.

"Could we talk about this later? Maybe over a drink?" Dallas gave Mary his phone. "Here, give me your number and

I'll text you."

"That's really nice of you." Mary typed in her number and handed the phone back.

Dallas pocketed it and gave them a wave as he left. "Don't let them wear you out too much, Mary."

"Okay, ladies, let's get started." She turned back to the class.

"You don't seem to mind that Bright can see right into the pool from his office," Glenda grumbled as she plopped into the water next to Lois.

"He's not a stranger though, is he?" Lois said.

Mary glanced up. Bright was in his office, looking right back at her. He was scowling as though she was on a strict timetable and not adhering to it. She gave him an awkward wave that he didn't return.

There hadn't been any more sightings of the enigmatic sock thief and it still remained a mystery as to who it was and why they had been stealing odd socks. However, this seemed to be the main topic of conversation when Mary walked into the lounge that afternoon for the residents' monthly meeting.

"All I'm saying," Lois said, "is that we don't know what they're going to take next. I've been hanging my washing on a rack inside and my living room is really too small for that."

Bright entered the room and everyone hurried to find seats. Mary sat down next to Helen.

"It's probably local hooligans, Lois," Glenda said. "I doubt they're interested in your underwear." She took the seat next to Jerry, beating Lois who had been heading that way. Lois scowled and went to sit on the other side of Mary.

"I've been keeping an eye on the video footage and there's been no unusual activity in the last few days," Bright said. He was wearing a crisp white shirt, the sleeves rolled up exposing his tanned forearms. "We've installed cameras outside the gates too and nothing suspicious has been recorded."

"I could get Dallas to have a look," Glenda said. "He's an electrician." She turned to Mary. "You could ask him when you go for drinks."

"That won't be necessary," Bright told her. "Like I said, cameras have been installed and I'm checking them often. Now, can we move on with the meeting?"

There was another five minutes of discussion as Viv, who was chairperson, welcomed them all and asked if everyone could see, which led to debate about which optometrist offered the best service. Then while going through the apologies, a further discussion as various ailments and illnesses were listed, along with talk of the Proctors' upcoming holiday in Noosa.

Mary could see that Bright was getting frustrated. They managed to get through three items on the agenda before Viv called for a break for afternoon tea. Klaus proposed that they add chocolate biscuits for the meetings to the agenda and Bright ran his hand through his hair until it was sticking straight up.

"Is it always like this?" he asked, as he poured himself a cup of coffee. "Don't have the tea," he added, as Mary reached for a cup and saucer. "Janice made it and it's not very good."

"It's not Janice's tea-making skills, it's the crap teabags she has to buy." Mary popped a sachet of peppermint tea into her cup. "I bring mine from home."

Bright took a SuperWine biscuit from the plate, went to take a bite and then seemed to change his mind. He cleared his throat. "It's probably none of my business, but I overheard Dallas on his phone earlier ..."

He was interrupted by Glenda who squeezed in between them to pour herself a coffee. "I'd be happy to bake a little something for next month's meeting. Gosh, I think even Lois could make better biscuits than these store-bought ones."

"That would be very welcome, I'm sure," Mary said.

"Some of those mince tarts would be good." Klaus had a cup with three biscuits balanced on the saucer.

"It won't be Christmas next month," Glenda said. "Mince tarts are only for December."

"Are they? I'll probably be on a diet by then," Klaus said.

"You could start now," Bright muttered.

Klaus ignored him and turned to Mary. "Could you take me to the supermarket some time? I need to buy some carrots."

"That would be a start," Bright said.

"They're not for me." He peered at Bright as though he had only just noticed him. "What are you doing here? Is it

Friday?"

"Oh, for ... Can we get on with this bloody meeting?"

It wasn't until later that Mary realised Bright had never said what it was that was none of his business.

CHAPTER 15

Nearly six million dollars are spent during the holiday season on ugly Christmas sweaters.

Bright

There was a ginger cat curled up on Bright's office seat when he arrived at Pacific Palms the next morning. With Dainty Dwellings closed, he'd got in earlier than usual. The cat must have been locked in overnight. It leapt off the chair and shot out the door.

"Tea?" Janice asked, poking her head through the door, handbag still hanging from her shoulder. "I'm going to make one for myself."

"Just a cup of hot water, thanks, Janice, I've brought my own," Bright told her, pulling out a bag from his pocket. "Don't worry about biscuits."

"Righto."

"Oh, and Janice?"

"Yes, boss?"

"We could probably splash out on better-quality tea. Maybe get some of those herbal ones too. I'll increase the budget a bit."

There was a host of maintenance issues to deal with and then he worked with Janice sorting out the bills that needed to be paid before the end of the year. They'd almost finished when Dallas stuck his head through the office door.

"Mornin', have you seen Mary anywhere?"

"I saw the van leaving five minutes ago. I believe she's taken some of the residents to the Botanic Gardens for an outing," Janice said.

"Oh, bugger." He reached into his pocket, then placed a sparkly star earring onto Janice's desk. "Can you give her this when you see her? Must have fallen off when we were eating breakfast."

Bright felt as if he'd been zapped with a cattle prod. Mary had slept with Dallas? After he'd told her that Dallas had a girlfriend. Only had he? He'd been meaning to, but then all the residents had these things to discuss, and no, he hadn't, he realised. Even so, it seemed rather quick, and he had thought that maybe ... although perhaps the attraction he had for Mary was one-sided? She was so friendly to everyone. The idea that she had been interested in him seemed foolish now. Of course she would go for someone like Dallas. He was fun and cheerful, not serious and drab like Bright.

He felt like an idiot imagining anything between him and Mary. They barely knew each other in any case. He would keep things professional from now on. Besides, he had too much else to worry about. Juggling his businesses, his father getting worse … well, that was all really … but still. It was enough.

Was Mary serious about Dallas? He should still mention the whole girlfriend thing to her, he decided. Any good friend would. It just went to show that first impressions were the most accurate though. He hadn't liked Dallas right from the beginning. What a cheating scumbag. Mary deserved better.

Right, to work. He would focus on making sure everything was running smoothly for Andrew's return. He opened up his emails.

"There's a terrible buzzing noise coming from the fridge in the bar," Dougal said, standing in the doorway with a scowl. "Something needs to be done about it."

"Are you sure it's not your hearing aid?" Bright asked.

"What's that?"

"I said it could be your hearing aid?"

"What could?"

"The noise you can hear." Bright held back a sigh.

"No, it's not my bleeding hearing aid." Dougal looked up to the heavens and rolled his eyes. "I don't even have the blasted thing turned on."

"Okay, I'll take a look at it when I get a moment," Bright said.

"You'll what?"

"Take a look at it when ..."

"Good. I'll come with you," Dougal said. "There's a few more things I want to go over."

"Oh, for fuck's sake," Bright muttered, getting up.

"Oi, watch your language," Dougal said. "You're not in the navy."

They made their way into the lounge where an old beer fridge sat behind the bar. The fridge was silent. They stood in front of it for an eternity, with Dougal shushing him every time he tried to speak.

"It'll start up again, wait ..."

"I don't think ..."

"Shhhhh."

There was a strange grumbling noise and then a *pffft*.

"That is odd," Bright said, "and it does smell like the gas might be leaking."

"Actually, that was me, not the fridge," Dougal admitted, looking a bit pink. "Cabbage last night. Or the beans this morning. Hard to say which."

"I'd imagine both," Bright said, looking around for a window to open. "In any case, the fridge seems fine. So I'd better head back to work ..."

"What about the other things?" Dougal asked. "There's an issue with the gardener ..."

"You know there's a monthly meeting for all this?" Bright said. "And the suggestion box?"

"I can't be arsed faffing around with the meeting. All those people going on about stupid bleedin' things of no importance."

"Hmmm." Bright raised one eyebrow.

"Besides," Dougal added, "*Days of Our Lives* is on then."

"Did your dad find you?" Janice asked when he got back to the office. "He came in looking for you and I sent him to the lounge."

"I didn't see him. I'll pop over shortly."

"Also, someone called Gary rang, asked if you wanted to 'play around'. I never knew you swung that way," Janice said with a wink.

Bright grinned. "My swing is excellent, Janice," he said, making her laugh.

"He wanted to meet at ten on Saturday at the golf club if you're keen." She flicked through some Post-it notes. "And your brother rang. Said it wasn't urgent and he'd call later."

He found Klaus at his kitchen table, a bowl of chips and another smaller one of nuts beside him. The table was covered in old maps of the world and Klaus had a ruler and a red pen that he was using to draw lines between various places. He was wearing a large green jumper that Bright imagined was far too hot for December. It was covered in glittery baubles and stars. It was hideous.

"It's a bloody long way to London," Klaus said when he saw Bright. "Almost fifteen centimetres."

Bright looked at his phone. It was almost one o'clock. Was it too early to have a drink?

Mary was swimming when Bright found her early the next morning. She had a strange, clumsy stroke, like a child, but she swam up and down continuously for at least fifteen minutes before she stopped, and seemed surprised to find him standing there when she was done. He hoped he didn't seem odd, wearing his suit pants and shirt in the steamy humidity of the indoor pool area, watching her swim.

"Good morning." She leant her elbows on the side of the pool and smiled up at him widely. "Are you coming in? It's lovely and warm again."

"Maybe later," he said, although he didn't really like swimming in pools. All that chlorine and the thought of other people's sweat in the water. He much preferred the ocean or, even better, a lake. "I wondered if I might have a quick word?" he added. "Non work-related."

"Well, darn, I was sort of hoping I'd get to see you shirtless," Mary joked, winking rather leerily. It was an odd thing to say to a friend, he thought.

"I'd have thought you might have seen more than enough of Dallas to be worrying about me in my smalls," he said. God, why had he said 'smalls'? Bloody old people and their lingo. His face flamed. Hers looked confused. "He has a girlfriend," he blurted out. He'd meant to say it a bit more gently than that but he was flustered.

"Who? Dallas?" Mary looked not the least bit worried by this information. "Yes, I know. I went to school with her. Although I wouldn't say we were close friends or anything. She was in the year below me."

"Well, even so, I don't think that's really very ... good. Of you." For crying out loud, he sounded like a prude. It was really none of his business who Mary was sleeping with, was it? And if she was sleeping with someone who had a girlfriend, that was on her. He should mind his own business.

"Sorry, Bright, but you've lost me," Mary said. "Was this what you wanted to talk to me about? Or was there something else?" She was getting out of the pool in those damn togs and Bright felt like an idiot for thinking someone so ... her ... would be interested in him.

"Never mind. It's not my business who you sleep with, or your moral compass. Forget I said anything."

"My moral ...? Who I ...?" Mary wrapped her towel around her waist. Her face had gone sort of stony looking. "Are you implying that I ... with Dallas? Knowing full well he had a girlfriend?" She was only tiny, but she looked rather ferocious. Bright felt an uncomfortable and untimely surge of lust go through him. "Albright Nicols, if you weren't my boss, I'd bloody well slap you, you idiot."

"Now hang on, I was only trying to help," he said. "As a friend." This seemed to make her madder.

"A friend? You think I'm your friend? A 'friend'," she made air quotes, "does not assume that their 'friend' — who, by the way was not thinking they were 'friends' — goes around sleeping with people when they already have a 'friend' they would much rather be 'friends' with!" She was yelling now, and all the air quotes were distracting him. It was hard to keep up with what she was saying. Was she mad he knew she was sleeping with Dallas? Or that Dallas had a girlfriend? All he could really establish was that she did not think of them as friends. Which made him feel rather crap actually.

"I'm very sorry, Mary," he said quietly. "Please forgive me for prying. It was really rather inappropriate of me. I'll let you get back to your swim."

Bloody chlorine, he thought as he left, making his eyes sting.

THE NEWSIE

Meditation classes are on today at 10 am in the rec room.

Anyone wanting a game of chess, the board will be set up in the library.

We will also be making Christmas tree decorations in the main hall at 11 am.
All welcome.

If you left an umbrella on the bus yesterday on the Botanic Gardens trip, please see Janice.

CHAPTER 16

Mary

When Mary got to work the next morning, she was still stewing over Bright's insinuation that she was sleeping with Dallas. Sure, Dallas was a nice guy. Good looking, easy to talk to and, all right, he was her usual type if she was honest. But she'd thought maybe there was something simmering with her and Bright and she was mad that he thought she was out there shagging guys with girlfriends.

She liked Bright. He had a softness about him, a hidden kindness behind his grumpy exterior. And he was good looking. All long limbs and smooth skin and lovely arms.

She and Dallas got on fine, and they'd met for breakfast, but there was no hot and heavy anything going on between them. The only thing they'd talked about was Akira, Dallas's girlfriend, and how he was thinking of proposing, and the equipment he was lending her for the Christmas party so they'd be able to play music. Why did Bright think she had slept with him?

As usual, she had too much to do. She found it so hard to leave work at work, and she was terrible at saying no to people.

The magician she'd hired for the party had called that morning to say he'd double booked. She should have kicked up a stink but instead she'd told him it was fine. So now she had the rest of the decorations still to be hung up, the catering to sort and some sort of entertainment to find, as well as all her regular jobs. Plus the van needed a warrant of fitness and she was supposed to be picking up a new pétanque set she'd found on Trade Me.

Not to mention, she really needed to re-dye her hair; the pink was faded right out to the edges now. Maybe she should just leave it its boring normal mousy blonde? Did she even have time for a day off between now and Christmas? She didn't normally work weekends but she had been going in on Saturdays to try to get on top of things. She was looking forward to doing the meditation class for a few minutes' peace.

There was a large group of residents in the rec room when she got there, all talking loudly over the top of each other. It was anything but calm. Lois was flapping her arms around like a chicken, yelling about tradition, while Glenda stood in front of her, hands on hips and her tongue out. Jerry was standing twisting his hands together.

"Ladies, really, I'm sure we can work this out ..." he said.

"She's doing it over my dead body," Lois said.

"That could be arranged," Glenda said, making Helen and Viv gasp in unison.

"What on earth is going on?" Mary asked. No one answered, the shouting getting louder. Lois started waggling a finger in Glenda's face and Glenda went to bite it. Helen and Viv leapt in to separate them, like prize boxers mid-match. There was a piercing whistle from the doorway.

"Oi! Knock it off in here. I can't even think and I lost my rook to a bloody pawn!" Dougal yelled.

It shut them up long enough for Mary to ask again what was happening.

"Mary will tell you," Lois said to Glenda, "I always put out the nativity display, don't I, Mary? Every year."

"But mine is better," Glenda said. "It's far better quality."

Lois reeled back like she'd been slapped. "How dare you? That set has been in my family for generations."

"Mine is from Smith and Caughey's," Glenda said haughtily.

"Oh, how lovely," said Janice as she walked in and Lois glared at her. "Sorry, don't mind me." She scuttled over to sit next to Klaus, who was perched with a plate of cheese and crackers, watching the drama unfold.

"I'm sure both sets are equally lovely," Mary said tactfully. "Surely we can come to a compromise, calmly and fairly."

"We should just use mine," Glenda said. "I'm sure everyone here is sick of the same old thing, year after year." She looked pointedly at Lois. "Something new and exciting would be better, don't you think, Jerry?"

Jerry was looking back and forward between the two ladies like he was watching a tennis match.

"Don't answer that, Jerry," Klaus muttered around a mouthful. "Trust me, there's a trap in there somewhere."

"I want to know why Dougal has to pawn anything," Bets said.

"Pawn or porn?" Sherry said with a giggle.

Mary felt decidedly like she'd had enough of the day. She hated conflict and she really didn't need anything else added to her pile of things to sort.

"How about we put both nativity scenes up?" she suggested.

"There can't be two baby Jesuses," Lois said, aghast.

"Or two virgin Marys," Glenda agreed.

"Well, technically," Viv said, "If she was a virgin, she didn't need Joseph, did she? To conceive."

"Or at all really," Helen said, nudging Viv.

"How about we put one in the main entrance and one by the tree?" Mary offered.

"Well, I suppose so," Lois said.

"Fine by me," Glenda nodded.

"Great, so shall we start the class?" Mary felt like no amount of meditation would help her relax now.

They all took their seats and Mary got out the CD player, taking a few deep, calming breaths. "I'm happy to report that we're very lucky to have Glenda's grandson Dallas bringing in some music equipment for Christmas," she said. "So we won't need to use this old thing."

"Oh, I almost forgot." Janice pulled something out of her pocket. "Dallas dropped this into the office yesterday while Bright and I were working. He said you left it at breakfast." She handed Mary her missing star earring.

"Ohhh, love is in the air," Sherry sang.

"Oh, I am pleased." Glenda clapped her hands. "I've never really liked that Akira. How wonderful. Mary and Dallas." She looked over at Lois and gave her a smug smile. "Just think, Mary for a possible daughter-in-law."

"For fuck's sake," Mary muttered under her breath. At least now she knew why Bright thought she was sleeping with Dallas.

"Mind your language," Dougal called from the other room. "You're not in the navy."

/ CHAPTER 17

People have been sending Christmas cards since 1842.

Bright

The cat was back. Bright tried shooing it away as he walked to his dad's but it followed him, meowing pathetically. He was a scrawny, ugly thing, half his tail was missing and one ear had a nick in it. He didn't look like a well-loved pet. Probably a stray.

Klaus was out in his garden, scattering cake crumbs onto a new bird feeder. He was in his pyjamas, his large belly poking out between the shirt and the pants, talking to himself.

He looks old, Bright thought, especially with his hair so long and his grey beard so unkempt.

"Morning, Dad," he called.

"Oh, hello there, just the person I was hoping to see," Klaus said, beaming. "I need you to take me shopping."

"What for?" Bright asked. He hoped it wasn't takeaways. Or chocolate.

"I need something from A Stitch in Time," Klaus told him.

"The sewing shop? What on earth do you need from there?"

"A bobbin. For the sewing machine."

"Mum's machine?" Bright clarified. "What on earth do you need a bobbin for? You don't even know how to sew."

"Ha! Shows what you know," Klaus said. "It's a bit tricky without the bobbin, but … get out of here, you mangy thing!" Klaus started waving his arms and making hissing noises. The ginger cat had come around the side of the house and was sitting beside the bird bath, leisurely licking its arse. "Bloody thing, it'll scare off the informants."

Bright sighed. "I'll ring animal control," he said. "When did you want to go to the shops?"

"After breakfast?" Klaus offered, rubbing his belly. "Or we could have something to eat there? That bakery next door does a good custard square."

"How about a haircut?" Bright suggested.

Klaus gave Bright a pat on the shoulder and smiled. "Good idea, you can do that while I get the food."

Klaus sent Bright into the bakery while he popped into the sewing shop. When Klaus came out he had several packages, neatly wrapped in brown paper, but he seemed in such a good mood Bright didn't want to ask what they were and spoil things.

"Did you get the bobbin?" he asked instead.

"Did you get the custard squares?" Klaus asked. "And the ham roll?"

"I did. Shall we eat them in the park? Then maybe we could both go and get a trim at the barber." Bright didn't really need it, but if that was what it took …

"I can't get a haircut," Klaus said. "Nobody will recognise me."

Bright wondered whether this was another symptom of dementia. Perhaps his dad's fear of forgetting who people were himself was making him worry people would forget him. He would have to ask Mary about it; she seemed to be quite knowledgeable. Then he remembered that Mary wasn't very happy with him and probably wouldn't want to be bothered with his questions.

Bern was about to take the kids to visit Santa when Bright rang him that evening.

"I'm leaving it a bit bloody late, I know," he said cheerfully. "Especially if they ask him for something we haven't got them. I took them last week but Tate was a bit scared of the old guy, so I thought we'd try again." There was a scuffling in the background. Bright could hear the two kids squabbling. "Hopefully he's better with him this time."

"Why don't you tell them Santa's not real?" Bright asked. "If they're scared of him, what's the point?"

"Fu...dge sake. They're a bit young for that. Imagine if Mum and Dad had told us at their age? Remember Mum dressing us in matching outfits and going down to the mall to tell Santa what we wanted?"

"Not really."

"I was always scared I hadn't been good enough. Dad's probably got the photos somewhere. You should ask him. How is the old bugger anyway?"

"Not great, to be honest. He's getting more forgetful and secretive. Then, when I think he's lost the plot, he seems almost back to his old self again."

"He seemed okay when I Skyped him last week. Except he asked the kids if they'd been good and told them he'd drop a little something off on Christmas Eve. Like he thought we lived down the road. Maybe he's getting the two of us muddled up."

"Dad," a voice whined in the background. "Are we going?"

"All right, hun, won't be a sec. Hey, I'd better get this lot in the car before they lose the plot." There was a pause on the line; neither of them had hung up. "I might bring the nippers over in the New Year. We don't know how long we've got left with him, do we?" Bern said quietly.

"It'd be great to see you anyway."

"Yeah, you too. Catch you later."

Bright took a can of beer from the fridge and sat in the shade on his back deck. He and his dad had built it together, right before Klaus had sold the family home and moved into the Palms. Even then he'd noticed his dad slowing down, but he'd still been fit from years of physical work and sharp as a tack. When they'd finished the job, they'd sat in this same place and cracked open a beer. Klaus had told Bright he should have got a wooden table, that the glass top wouldn't age well. He'd been right. It had dulled over time and there was a large crack on the edge where his niece had whacked it with something. Bern and Di's last visit had been two years ago, Bright realised. It would be good to see them again. If his mum had been alive, she'd never have let that much time pass without seeing her grandchildren.

It was no use feeling maudlin though. He'd go for a quick run before it got too dark and have a shower, then cook dinner for one.

While he ran, Bright wondered what Mary was doing. Was she out with Dallas? Or was he at her place? The zebra light would be casting a soft glow over the room. Did she have the same music playing? Were they laughing and drinking wine, because Dallas wouldn't have to drive home?

He should find someone to go on a date with. Gary might know someone, or he could try those online dating apps. But his mind was adrift, thinking of a diminutive, pink-haired lady, with sparkly earrings and a wide smile, and he was pretty damn certain that he'd missed the boat.

THE NEWSIE

Final numbers needed for the annual Christmas party by the end of the week, please.

Spaces are filling up for Carols in the Park, but we still have a few seats left in the van. Please let Mary know ASAP if you'd like to come along.

A reminder that the maintenance and gardening teams will be taking a break over the festive period, so if you have any requests, get them in now.

And a very happy 80th birthday to Brian Carson. We all hope you had a lovely lunch outing with your daughter yesterday.

CHAPTER 18

Mary

"Could you pop this in Dougal's cubby?" Janice grimaced and held out a white envelope to Mary. "I was going to give it to him earlier when he was in the library reading the paper but I lost my nerve. He doesn't get much mail, does he?"

Mary took the envelope from her and turned it over to look at the back. There was a name, neatly written in block letters, but no return address. "It's from his daughter in England," she said. "I'll take it down to him."

"I didn't know Dougal had a daughter."

"Rachel. He doesn't hear from her much." She waved the envelope. "Just this."

The doors and windows to Dougal's house were closed and the sheer curtains to the living room were drawn shut. Dougal said it was to preserve the furniture which, to be fair, was in very good condition. He never had visitors and Mary hadn't often been invited inside, only when there was a maintenance issue he wanted to show her. It was either stifling hot or cold and gloomy, depending on the time of year.

Dougal came to the door, sighing as he saw her. "Oh, it's you."

"Hello, Dougal," she said cheerfully. "Mail for you."

Dougal took the envelope, turned it over and read the name on the back and grunted. He tucked the card inside his cardigan.

"I thought you were the manager," he said. "He's meant to be coming to have a look at the wallpaper in my sitting room. The glue they used was substandard. Maybe you could have a look? I've been waiting for hours."

"And I'm here now." Bright came up behind Mary, making her jump. "I can assure you that you've been top priority, Mr Cartwright."

He was standing so close Mary could smell his aftershave, or maybe it was body wash. It was fresh and citrusy. It probably lingered in the bathroom after he'd showered … Then she remembered how he'd jumped to conclusions about Dallas. "I'll leave you to enjoy your card, Dougal," she said, and stepped sideways to avoid colliding with Bright.

"Enjoy? The bloody insolence! What's it to you what I do with my mail?" Dougal barked. He leant closer to Mary. Beads of spit had formed on his lips. "Why don't you mind your own flaming business and stop interfering in everyone else's?"

"Now, Dougal ..." Bright started.

"Mr Cartwright!" Dougal bellowed. He turned back to Mary. "Nobody wants to be your friend. You work here. That's it. Take your ridiculous earrings and stupid candyfloss hair and piss off. Find some friends your own age."

"Mr Cartwright, I don't think ..."

Mary felt her face flush and tears blurred her eyes. She turned and ran down Dougal's front path, not waiting to hear what Bright was saying.

She'd always been a bit of a loner and apart from Patsy, had found it hard to make friends. When she'd lived with her mum they'd moved so much, she'd never stayed at one school for an entire year. They'd never had a house she'd wanted to invite other children back to and she'd felt disapproval rolling from the other mothers. Mary was the little girl in the too-big or too-small charity shop clothes. Bare feet and walking home alone. Party invitations never came her way, or invitations to play or for sleepovers.

Later, Gran had been her best friend, and she'd told Mary she was an old soul. When Gran had a group of friends over to play cribbage or for craft evenings, she'd loved listening to their stories about the old days. The moving around might have meant she hadn't done that well in school in her primary years, but she'd learnt a lot of the skills she used now at the village from Gran.

Even though she was doing her job, Mary did consider the residents her friends. They drove her mad sometimes, but she knew about their families and grandchildren, ailments and fears. They laughed over silly mishaps and shared a glass of wine or a gin and tonic from time to time. To think that she was only seen as an employee hurt. But she reminded herself that Dougal was hurting as well. It came from a place of guilt and regret. There Mary was, every day, yet he hadn't seen his own daughter for over thirty years. There was no way to contact her or make amends, even if he wanted to.

Mary tried to compose herself as she walked back to the clubhouse. She had bingo to run that afternoon and needed to make sure the 'Peppy Puzzlers' had packed up from their morning get-together. There was also the podiatrist to call to book a final visit for the residents before the end of the year and she needed to check with the cafeteria that there were enough wine glasses and crockery for the Christmas party.

"Mary, love, slow down." Turning, she found Lois power-walking in her direction and stopped to wait, plastering a smile on her face, but it felt forced.

Lois finally caught up and when she saw Mary's face she reached out and touched her arm, eyebrows drawn together with concern. "Are you all right, love? Have you been crying?"

"It must be the pollen," Mary sniffed. "It's terrible at this time of year."

Lois raised her eyebrows. "Nonsense. There's no fooling me, my darling. How about a chat and a cup of tea?"

"I really don't have time."

"Nobody's dying, are they? Come on, twenty minutes tops. I'll bet you haven't even had lunch yet. I've baked cheese scones, but I'm sure Jerry won't notice a couple missing."

Mary hadn't eaten lunch and her stomach grumbled. "That does sound nice ..."

"And I've got an idea for centrepieces for the tables. Do you have a theme in mind? Glenda was talking to Bets about red candles but I thought white and silver might be more classy."

Lois chattered on as they walked and Mary found herself seated at Lois's kitchen counter, a heavily buttered scone and cup of Earl Grey in front of her, despite her protests.

"Can I ask you something?" She took a bite of her scone.

"Of course, my darling, you can ask me anything. We're friends, aren't we?"

That almost made Mary cry again. "Never mind." She swallowed her mouthful and the lump that had lodged in her throat. "Tell me about your idea."

"Better still, I'll show you."

Lois scurried off into her spare bedroom and came back with an armful of white and silver fabric flowers. She'd arranged them perfectly on wire circles. "I've made a few of these up — one for each table — and painted glass jars silver with white candles for the middle."

Mary's eyes welled up again.

"Oh, my darling, you don't have to use them. I thought it might be helpful but I won't be offended ..."

"No, they're perfect. Thank you, Lois. You've no idea how much this means to me."

Lois patted her hand. "That's what friends are for. Now finish your scone, you've already gone over your break time."

THE NEWSIE

For those who have been asking about meal choices, the Christmas dinner will be a buffet this year, so no need to choose an option.

The podiatrist will be here on the 20th. Please see Mary or Janice if you haven't yet booked a time. There are still some spots left.

Marlene will be here on the 22nd for those wanting their hair set and she also has two appointments left for nails on the 23rd at her salon.

CHAPTER 19

Mary

Helen answered the door wearing a silky dressing gown. Her hair was a bit knotted.

"Sorry, did I wake you from a nap?" Mary asked. "Only I was wondering if you'd spoken to Ada?"

"Not today, no. Viv?" Helen called down the hallway. "When did you last see Ada?"

Viv came into sight, wrapped in a towel.

"Hello, Mary love, I dropped her off some soup yesterday," she said. "Why?"

Mary shook her head. "It's probably nothing, but I promised to drop her off some more envelopes for her Christmas cards and she's not answering the door. She might be napping too."

Helen and Viv exchanged a look.

"Ada never naps. Says she can't sleep at night if she does." Helen beckoned Mary inside. "She gave me a key for emergencies. I'll see if I can find it."

"I'll throw my clothes back on," Viv said. "I hope she's all right."

Mary waited while Helen searched the kitchen draw for the key. Helen and Viv had a lovely home. It was full of artwork and knick-knacks they'd collect on their travels over the years. There was a fancy coffee maker on the bench and the place smelt of patchouli.

"Here it is," Helen said, holding up a key ring with a luggage tag attached. "I don't know why that's on here, not like I don't know her address."

The soup was sitting on the kitchen bench untouched when Mary entered Ada's house. It was musty and strangely eerie, the curtains still closed and the hum of the fridge the only noise.

"Yoo hoo, Ada?" she called, but in her heart she knew what she was going to find.

Ada was still in bed, her long grey hair plaited down one side of her neck, her quilt tucked up around her armpits and her teeth in a glass beside the bed.

Mary reached out and touched her forehead. It was cold.

"Oh, Ada," she said, stroking her face gently.

Outside, Helen and Viv were waiting.

"Is she all right?" Viv asked.

Mary shook her head, the lump in her throat making it hard to talk. "She's gone," she said, trying not to cry.

Viv put a hand over her mouth. Helen put an arm around her. "Oh no, and right before Christmas. Poor Ada."

The last thing Mary wanted to do was talk to Bright, but Janice wasn't at her desk and she had to tell someone about Ada. Family would need to be rung, and the funeral home called. She knocked on his door, her hand a bit shaky.

"Come in," he called.

"Only me," she said, her voice wobbly. He was at his desk, hair a bit wild like he'd been running his hands through it.

"Mary," he said, and something about the way he said her name made her want to cry. She swallowed hard. "Please, come in. I'm so sorry about the way Dougal spoke to you. I intend to have words with him about it and, oh God, please don't cry."

Was she crying? She wiped at her wet face, then opened her mouth to speak and a sob came out. Bright came around the desk and his big arms wrapped around her, his chest warm as he enveloped her. It was lovely and she let herself cry.

"Please don't let him upset you," Bright said. "He's an arse. Everyone here thinks you're wonderful. I think you're wonderful. I like the hair. And the weird earrings."

Mary realised Bright thought she was still upset about Dougal. And she'd snotted all over his lovely pale-blue shirt. She pulled reluctantly away. "I'm not upset about Dougal," she said. "I mean, I was, but I know why he's like that. It's not him, it's Ada."

He looked at her blankly. "Ada Greene? She's at number thirty-two." He nodded and raised one eyebrow slightly. "I'm afraid she's passed away," Mary said, and started to cry again.

CHAPTER 20

Christmas pudding originally had meat in it.

In the 14th century, Christmas pudding was a type of porridge made using mutton and beef with spices, wines, raisins and currants. Over time, people slowly added more alcohol alongside eggs and dried fruit until we eventually ended up with the Christmas pudding we're all familiar with today.

Bright

Everyone was talking about Ada by the time Bright had made all the appropriate calls and Mary had stopped crying. He'd suggested they go to the cafe for a cup of tea and the place was packed with residents.

"And then all my lights flickered on and off," Sherry said. "I'll bet it was about when she went. What time would you say that was, Dale?"

"It was six-fifteen," Dale said. "I know, because I'd gotten up to take my pill, and the alarm clock went all funny and then reset itself."

"My lights flickered too," Glenda said. "It woke me up. I thought it was an electrical storm." She shuddered rather theatrically. "It was terribly frightening."

Lois did a little snort. "I was already up. I like to get up early, not laze around. It's the best part of the day if you ask me."

"But did your lights flicker?" Sherry asked.

"They did. Do you suppose it was Ada?" Lois asked. "I don't like to think of her as a ghost though."

Dougal snorted. "Bunch of hokey," he said.

"Do you think her emergency button was working?" Bets asked.

"When my Max died, he used to communicate with me," Raylene said. "I'd say, is that you, Max? Are you there? And he'd be listening and send me a sign."

"Poppycock," Dougal said. "He never listened to a word you said when he was alive, why would he start now when he could finally have some peace and quiet?"

Several people gasped and Raylene's face fell.

"All right, Dougal, that's it," Bright said firmly. He'd had enough of the old bugger. "I think you've upset enough people for one day. I'm going to ask you to leave for now."

Dougal frowned. "You can't order me to leave," he said

indignantly, "I bleeding well live here."

"Not for much longer if you can't treat people with a bit of respect," Bright told him. "There are rules, and you signed a contract when you moved in. Now I suggest you spend twenty-four hours having a break from everyone, and maybe offer some apologies to the people you've upset."

"Well, I never," Dougal said, but he got up from the table and didn't look anyone in the eye as he left the cafe.

❄

"Wonderful news," Janice said, passing him on her way in, "Nat and Andy have had the babies."

Mary started to cry again. Bright looked at her in concern and she laughed, waving her hands to fan her face.

"Sorry," she said, "happy tears this time."

"Don't be too harsh on Dougal," Mary said over tea and a muffin. "It's a hard time of year for him."

Bright thought Mary was far too nice. "He's a grumpy old fart."

"Yes, but he has his reasons."

Mary told him about Dougal's wife and daughter Rachel. How he had no way to contact her, or his grandchildren who he had never met. It *was* sad, Bright had to admit.

"Have you noticed he doesn't drink?" Mary said. "He gave up after they left. I've never seen him touch a drop." Bright hadn't really noticed. "He even went over to London years ago, trying to find them, but no luck. Christmas for him is a sad time. He gets Rachel's card and it reminds him of what he lost. It makes him extra cantankerous."

"Even so, he can't speak to you like that," Bright said. "He really upset you."

"It's okay. Normally I don't let him get to me. I think I was just feeling a bit overwhelmed by everything, with the lead-up to Christmas. He's usually not so bad."

Bloody hell, Bright thought. That could be him in a few years' time. A grumpy old man who turns into the Christmas Grinch and makes people cry. He didn't want to become Dougal.

But there wasn't much he could do about the Christmas budget. Andrew had made a few errors over the year with some of the residents' funeral bills and Bright didn't want to contact the families to try to get money out of them. It was a bad look for Pacific Palms and it seemed like a crappy thing to do. But that money had to come from somewhere and the only way he could see to recoup the loss was to cut the party budget down.

"Look, about the Christmas party," he said. Mary looked up at him, hope in her eyes. "Perhaps I could help with some of the prep work?"

Mary gave him a small smile. "Sure, yeah, that would be great. Thanks." She sounded tired and less bubbly than normal. He felt awful.

"What can I do?"

"Any chance you know how to make a Christmas pudding?" He didn't. "I'll give you Gran's recipe. You can't go wrong."

You could. He used Klaus's kitchen since the hob was bigger than his. Mary had already soaked the fruit in brandy for the last week, so he'd gathered up the rest of the ingredients and after dinner he got to work.

He'd thought Klaus might object, since he was not a fan of Christmas things, but he seemed pleased at the idea of helping. Probably thinking of his ever-expanding stomach.

'Cream the sugar and butter, then add in the eggs one by one,' he read. Seemed simple enough.

An hour later, Bright looked around in dismay. Every surface was covered in a layer of flour. Blobs of fruit mix covered the splashback, the hob and even the toaster. He'd burnt his hand on the hot calico cloth and his puddings all had strange lumpy bulges. There were three. One hadn't made it. It sat on the floor in a pile that looked a little like dog vomit.

Still, they smelt quite good, boiling away in their pots. Bright just had to hope he hadn't stuffed them up. He set to work, cleaning up. Klaus was still sitting on the sofa where he'd been observing the whole time and making helpful comments like 'Are you sure that's what the recipe said?' and 'Bloody hell, it looks a bit of a dog's breakfast.'

"Have you fed the cat, Dad?" Bright asked.

"Yes, she had one of those sachet things." Klaus looked up at him and tilted his head slightly. "Is it Friday then?" he asked.

It actually was, Bright realised with a grin.

CHAPTER 21

It's very rare to be born on December 25th — Christmas Day is the least likely day of the year to be born, whereas studies suggest that there's a higher chance of dying on Christmas, the day after Christmas or New Year's Day than any other single day of the year.

Bright

They took the van to the church for the funeral. Any of the residents who didn't drive lined up to get in, a process that seemed to take longer that the actual drive there, with walkers and canes piling up in the back and everyone discussing hip replacements and their various types of arthritis.

Mary, he discovered, rode a bike to work. She had her gran's car, she told him, but she only used it if she had to.

Things were a bit awkward with them. He wasn't sure if it was because of the whole Dallas thing, or the hug he probably shouldn't have given her. Maybe he was imagining it.

The service seemed to take a long time. It was stinking hot inside the chapel and Bright was sweltering in his suit jacket and tie. Mary wore a dark navy dress and had her hair pulled back in a short ponytail at the base of her neck. She looked different. Nice, but more normal than he'd ever seen her. Bright wasn't sure he liked it.

Ada's family had come from out of town, so Mary and Janice had organised afternoon tea in the cafeteria afterwards. Bright found a seat next to Klaus, who had a cup of tea and a plate with a club sandwich, a scone and two biscuits balanced on his knee.

"All right, Dad?" He took one of the biscuits and Klaus switched the plate to his other knee.

"Wasn't it a lovely service?" Klaus said.

Glenda had sat down on his other side. "Not a very good turnout though," she said. "When my Raymond died, I counted one hundred and twenty-three."

"We had over two hundred at Jack's funeral," Lois called out from across the way. "I thought that was pretty good as we'd only moved to the city five years beforehand. There was so much food left over and still people were leaving casseroles on my doorstep for weeks."

"I did all the catering myself for Raymond. It took my mind off the grief."

Viv was listening in. "My husband and I divorced after seven years, but when he dies I'll dance on his grave. Miserable git."

"I didn't know you were married, Viv," Lois said.

"Biggest mistake of my life." Viv smiled over at Helen.

"Jack and I had a wonderful forty-five years together, and I'd do it all again," Lois said.

Jerry's cup rattled against the saucer as he picked it up. "I would too," he said.

"Well, weddings are fine, but I do love a good funeral," Glenda said firmly. Several people nodded in agreement.

Bright watched Mary as she chatted to each resident, offering a hug or a tissue when needed. She'd cried during the service and her eyes were still red. Each loss must be hard for her as she got to know everyone so well. She seemed so kind and it surprised him that she was the type of woman who would go after a man who would cheat. Or that she'd be willing to hurt someone herself. But maybe he didn't have all the facts and it was something mutually agreed.

He ditched work early to meet up with Gary for a game of twilight golf.

"Mate," Gary said on the seventh hole, "you're playing like shit."

Bright watched as his ball hit a tree and landed in the long grass somewhere underneath it. "It's been a day," he said.

"Looking forward to a drink after this, to tell you the truth."

Gary and Bright had known each other since university. They were in neighbouring dorm rooms and the next year, even though Gary had left and gotten a construction job, they flatted together. When Bright had finished his business degree it was Gary who suggested he and Bern should invest the money his mother had left them in the retirement village.

Years later, after Gary got back from a stint living in Europe, he'd asked Bright if he wanted to partner up on a business idea. And Dainty Dwellings was born. They worked well together, Gary doing more of the manual work and him in administration. He was trying to do the marketing too, but he was thinking they might have to start hiring out for that. And take on another building apprentice.

Bright had been best man at Gary and Sharon's wedding and was a godfather to his three kids. Apart from Bern, Gary was his best friend.

"Did I tell you Sharon's mum broke her bloody leg," Gary said, putting his tee down and balancing his golf ball on top. "Fell over that stupid rat of a dog of theirs and cracked her fibula."

"Shit, that's no good," Bright said, looking for his water bottle in his bag. "How's she going to cope?"

"Sharon's going to stay on after Christmas and help her," Gary said. "But we're going to have to move Christmas to her place now." He took a swing, watching with satisfaction as it flew down the fairway. "Bloody pain in the arse. I'd already booked the marquee for our place but the bird at the hire place tells me it's too late for a refund."

"Bugger," said Bright, pulling his trundler down the fairway with a sigh. "When will you head off?"

"Christmas morning," Gary said. "Less traffic, and then we don't have to try to smuggle all the kid's stocking stuff into the car."

"Makes sense," Bright agreed. "Bloody Christmas, eh?"

Gary gave him a long look. "What's up? Is it your dad?"

"No. Well, yes, him too. He's definitely getting more doolally. I think he forgets he's eaten and then he eats again. He's getting fatter every time I see him. And he's a bit away with the fairies most days. Gets strange ideas about things and insists they're important. But he seems okay in terms of taking care of himself. He showers, dresses himself, hasn't left the oven on or anything."

"Well, that's something. What does Bern say?"

"Well, he only hears what I tell him really. He's busy — he's got the kids, Di's working long hours, and he's back part time now too. I dunno. Not much he can do from Perth, is there?"

"No, but if you have to make decisions at some point, it shouldn't be all on you."

Bright stared glumly down at his ball, sitting precariously near a water hazard.

"Let's hope that's not too soon," he said, contemplating which club to use.

"So if it's not your dad, what's making you so miserable?" Gary asked. "I'd use your seven iron if I were you."

Bright pulled out the club and tried to find some balance on the edge of the water.

"It's this woman at work," he said. "Mary."

"Ahh, what? One of the oldies' kids? Not another bloody accountant, is she?" Gary pulled out his phone and fiddled around with the screen.

"She's not actually. She works there. And she's nothing like any other woman I've dated." He looked up. "You'd better not be filming me," he said, and Gary grinned.

"Just in case it's a miracle shot. Or a good laugh." Bright gave him the finger. "So what's wrong with her then, this Mary?"

Bright swung, hitting the ball onto the edge of the green where it rolled back and into the water.

"Shit, bad luck, mate," Gary laughed.

"Nothing's wrong with her," Bright said. "She's amazing. And cute and quirky. But she's seeing someone."

"Shit. Now that is bad luck," Gary said.

THE NEWSIE

Exciting news for those who haven't yet heard — Natalie and Andrew have welcomed two lovely baby boys into the world! Zayn Andrew and Bodie Benjamin weighed seven pounds one and six pounds nine and Mum and babies are doing well. Janice will be taking flowers and our gift to the maternity ward and we look forward to meeting the newborns soon. If you haven't signed the card, it needs to be done by 4 pm.

The craft session today will be making our own Christmas crackers for the party. Bring your best (clean) jokes please to the rec room at 2 pm.

A quick reminder to make sure you are slip, slop, slapping over these warm summer months. Sunscreen and hats will help, and staying out of the midday heat.

We will be booking in a mole check visit in April. Also, please remember, nude sunbathing is not permitted at the Palms.

CHAPTER 22

Mary

The tyre was flat on Mary's bike. She swore under her breath as she bent to examine it. A fifteen-minute bike ride home would now take her almost an hour to walk.

"Need a ride?"

She squinted up to see Dallas, elbow hanging out the open window of a black ute. "That would be great, I'm only down the road. Are you sure you wouldn't mind?"

"Yeah, nah, no problem." He hopped out and together they lifted the bike onto the flat deck. Mary climbed gratefully into the passenger seat. Dallas was blocking the road. Bright had pulled up behind them in his silver BMW, tapping his fingers on the steering wheel.

"Is this a new car?" Mary asked.

"It's my dad's. He's retired so he doesn't use it much any more. They have a Honda Fit which is great for round town and uses less gas, so he lets me use this when I'm here."

"Did you say you were looking for a job?" Mary clicked her seatbelt and Dallas started to drive sedately, sticking to the twenty-kilometres-per-hour speed limit. He gave Bright a little wave through the rear-vision mirror.

"Yeah, Akira's keen to move back. She's from here too and she's going to set up a beauty salon from home, so it's me that needs to find a job. Probably not the best time of year to be looking." He turned out of the village and increased to a normal speed. "You'll need to give me directions."

Mary made a quick stir-fry and sat at her kitchen table with her laptop, trying to fit all the activities she had planned into the following week's calendar. She'd really have to stop saying yes to everything the residents asked her. It would be nice to have more of a social life too. Perhaps when Dallas and Akira had settled in, she'd have them over for dinner? Dougal might be an old grouch but he was right; she did need some more friends her own age.

Her phone dinged with a text. It was Patsy reminding her about the parcel deliveries. She'd forgotten about that but sent back a thumbs-up emoji. She'd make it work somehow.

"Oof, my hip's playing up again. Could you give me a hand up, love?"

Mary helped Lois up from her yoga mat. "You know, you

can do this from a chair if you want. Like Francine and Glenda do."

"When I get to their age, maybe I will," Lois said. Mary recalled that Glenda was only three years older, although Francine had a few more years on them than that.

"I think it was all the sitting at Ada's funeral. I just need to get moving. Might get on my exercycle tonight."

"Cycling is great exercise. And you can go as slow as you need to."

"Speaking of cycling, I noticed that Dallas chap picked you up from work yesterday. Glenda is almost beside herself with glee that he's been courting you." Lois's mouth puckered as though she'd bitten a lemon.

"Dallas? No, we're not dating. He gave me a ride home because I had a flat tyre. I'm sure he's a nice guy, but he has a girlfriend."

Lois's face lit up. "Well, that's great news." She waved to Viv and Helen who had packed up their belongings and were on their way out. "I've been meaning to say, love, I'm so sorry you were the one who found Ada. It must have been a bit of a shock."

"It was. I haven't been first on the scene before, though I suppose it had to happen sometime. Part of the job. Bright was lovely though. I thought he'd think I was being a big sook but he didn't at all. I got snot all over his shirt too."

"I have to say, I'm getting quite used to him. He even gave me a smile the other day. And he dresses so nicely. Do you think he irons his own shirts? He doesn't have a wife, does he?"

"No, I don't think so."

Lois gave Mary a little nudge. "Well, he's very good looking. And now that you're not dating that Dallas ..."

"He seems very nice, but I'm sure he's far too busy controlling you lot to be thinking about any of that."

"You could always offer to iron his shirts for him. That's a good way to show a man you're taken by him."

"I'm not taken by him." Mary's face felt warm all of a sudden. "Now get out of here so I can tidy up."

Bright *was* probably too busy. He was running two businesses, and Mary could barely manage to organise the activities for eighty residents. The women he dated were probably the super-organised type. Career women. They'd schedule outings and dinners to fit in with both their hectic lifestyles. Maybe even sex was slotted in, twice a week; a weekend evening and one other day. An image thrust itself into her head of rolled-up shirt sleeves and muscled arms. She couldn't imagine limiting herself to set nights of the week if she was Bright's girlfriend.

Lois was standing on a chair in the entrance to the rec room, with Bets hovering nearby as though she was going to save her if she fell, when Mary came in to use the computer the next afternoon.

"Lois, please be careful," she said. "That doesn't look safe." They would be sued, she thought, if she fell and broke a hip. "What are you ladies up to?"

"Some of us have noticed," Lois puffed, "that you've been as busy as a little worker bee."

"… or a blue-arsed fly," Bets added.

"And we thought we'd give you a hand with the decorating. You always make everything so nice for us. Look at this as our way to show our appreciation."

Mary gazed around the lounge. There was tinsel hanging from every available shelf, knick-knacks on the tables and clumps of mistletoe above each doorway. "Well, thank you. It looks very festive." It would help with the budget as well. She might even be able to splurge on some ingredients to make Christmas fudge.

"Have either of you seen Dougal over the last couple of days?" Mary understood why Bright had told him to go away. Mostly the residents tolerated his crotchety nature but he'd been especially rude. She wanted to make sure he was all right though. It would be uncomfortable for both of them, after their last encounter, and she realised she'd been avoiding it.

"He was in the library earlier reading the paper," Bets said. "Apparently they need to use a larger print and he's going to write a letter to the Editor to tell them so."

There was no need to go and check on him then. He was obviously back to his normal self.

Lois climbed carefully down from the chair and observed their handiwork.

"Well. It does look good, if I must say so myself. What do you think, Bets, shall we get Bright to come and have a look?"

"He's not in the office," Janice said, overhearing as she went past. "But it looks wonderful, ladies. I'll be sure to tell him to have a look when he gets back."

Lois and Bets went off, nattering about their costumes for the Christmas party.

"Make sure you tell Bright we expect everyone to dress up," Lois called.

Janice snorted. "Good luck with that."

Mary wondered, if he had been the dressing-up type, which he clearly wasn't, what kind of costume he might wear.

CHAPTER 23

One in three men wait until Christmas Eve
to do their shopping.

Bright

He was still an arsehole, Bright thought, as he watched Dallas help Mary lift her bike onto the back of his truck.

If he had been a violent man, he'd punch that smug look off his face.

They both knew what they were doing, no doubt, but he couldn't help but feel slightly disappointed in Mary, and something else as well that he couldn't put his finger on.

He still hadn't remembered to book in a locksmith to have a look at Klaus's garage. Bright was hoping they would find the key to the car inside, although he wasn't sure how his dad could have managed that. But the car was a bit of a mess, covered in a layer of pollen and poo and pōhutukawa petals. Maybe he could try to hose it off and put a cover over it in the meantime?

The cat was back, meowing at his office window, and Bright realised he'd never rung animal control. He could do that in the morning, but the poor thing was looking a bit miserable and Bright couldn't look at its eyes, pleading with him through the glass any longer.

"I just have to pop out for a meeting," he told Janice, grabbing his keys and tucking his phone into his back pocket. He felt a bit stupid making up a story, but would feel even more stupid admitting he'd gone down to the pet store. It was only as he pulled up outside the shop that he realised he could have taken some of Holly's food from his dad's house. He really was distracted.

He had a bowl, a water feeder, some grain-free cat biscuits and three different pouches of fancy food for the bloody thing, and now he found himself standing in the aisle looking at toys. This was ridiculous; it was a mangy old stray. It didn't need a bloody feather-tailed mouse on a stick. He made himself put it back.

When they were kids, they'd begged and begged for a pet. Eventually his parents had caved in and they'd got kittens. One tabby each. His was called Penelope and Bern's was Brains since they were big on *Thunderbirds* at the time. They had them about two weeks before his mum had to rehome them. Bern, it turned out, was highly allergic. They got fish after that, until Bern left home, and Klaus inherited Holly from a neighbour.

He got a cage and a blanket for the cat. Not because he planned to keep the bloody thing, but more to help catch it. Then he could drop it off somewhere, wherever you took cats. The pound, or the SPCA or whatever.

He should do some shopping for gifts while he was at the mall. Buy his dad something. He usually put money in an account for Bern's kids, but maybe he could get them a gift. It might still get to them in time if he posted it today.

Everyone was out at the shops. It was chaos. There was a long line of parents with kids, waiting for their photo to be taken with the mall Santa. Bright thought he looked nothing like he should. He had a patently fake fur beard and he was too skinny. It made him think of his dad, dressed up in that suit, pretending for the sake of a wife he'd adored.

Bern had gotten married to his childhood sweetheart too. He'd been so sure, so convinced that Di was it for him. Just like his parents. Bright had never met anyone who he'd felt like that about. Never met anyone he could imagine being with forever, having kids with, dressing up as Santa for.

He wondered if Mary thought Dallas was 'the one'. If she wanted marriage and kids and pets. He wasn't even sure why he was even thinking about that, about Mary.

Would it be weird to get her a gift? Probably. But he could maybe get her something little? Some fun earrings or something? He could decide later if he even gave them to her. What would Dallas give her? Would he spend the day with her? Or with his other girlfriend?

He wandered around the shops, battling the crowds, and finally found a gag gift for Gary and a board game for his kids, and some toys for Bern's. He got his dad a book and some aftershave, and Bern and Di some funny socks, and then went to the post office. The wait was horrendous. There was a queue out the door of fed-up-looking shoppers with parcels. He decided he'd pop down to the one near his house the next day.

By the time he got back to the Palms, the back of his car was full of shopping.

"Can I help you with any of that?" Lois offered as he lugged the pet supplies in the door.

"No, no, I'm fine thanks, Lois," he said.

"It's no trouble," Lois insisted, tugging on a bag.

"Really, I can cope," he told her, gently tugging back. She tugged harder.

"Go on, let me help, we oldies like to be useful." She took the bag and peered inside, rummaging around rather noisily. "What have you been buying?"

"Nothing," Bright said, not wanting to admit to anything cat related. "Just some things for Dad."

"Aren't you a good boy?" Lois reached across for an awkward — for him at least — pat on his bottom.

They made it rather slowly to his office and he put the

bags down next to his desk.

"Thank you so much for your help, Lois," he said, taking the bag off her.

"Absolutely no problem." She fiddled with her handbag and hitched it up her shoulder. "Perhaps I'll see you at the Christmas movie?"

"I'm not really a Christmas movie fan."

Lois put her hand over her heart. "Oh, Bright, how can you say that? Maybe you haven't seen the right one yet?" She gave him a little smile and with a pat of her handbag she was off.

Right. On to the locksmith he thought, checking the files for contact details of someone they had used before. He wrote the number down and then picked up his desk phone to punch it in. The receiver made an odd beeping sound and then the dial tone came back. He tried hanging up and starting again, but it was the same.

He'd have to use his mobile. But it wasn't in his pocket. Perhaps he'd popped it into one of the shopping bags? It wasn't there either. Odd. It must be in the car, he thought.

The cat was now nowhere to be seen.

THE NEWSIE

We have another Christmas movie marathon
happening this Sunday.

It's a Wonderful Life is on at 10 am,

The Polar Express at 2 pm and

Elf at 6 pm.

Apologies to those who wanted Die Hard
and Bad Santa, but they were deemed not
appropriate by management.

CHAPTER 24

Mary

The popcorn machine was on the fritz. Mary had tried unplugging it and pushing the reset button, but it wasn't heating up. It was a fairly old one that someone's family member had donated but it made lovely buttery snacks for the residents while they watched movies in the cinema. Normally, anyway. It had worked fine for the earlier morning film but now was refusing to cooperate.

"Sorry, Helen, I'm afraid it will have to be chips from the bar or something." She gave the machine an irritated thump. It made a slight clicking sound and then it started. "What the ..."

"You're like the Fonz with the jukebox," Viv said.

"I always liked his girlfriend, Leather Tuscadero," Helen said. Mary had no idea what they were talking about. The machine started to do its thing so she left them to it and went into the cinema to have a quick clean-up from the previous movie.

The cinema was a small room at the end of the hallway, with no windows and thirty tiered seats, each with a cup holder. She checked those first. The residents often left things behind in them: tissues, hearing aids, even false teeth. Once, like something in a horror movie, she'd found Leonard Parson's glass eye, staring up at her from the plastic cavity.

"Lois said you were looking for me?" Bright said, striding into the room. He was so tall and efficient looking in his crisp shirt. It was a pale-lavender one today, she noted.

"No, I don't think so?" She avoided looking at his arms where the shirt sleeves were rolled up again.

"She said it was an emergency?"

The door clicked shut behind him, casting the room into darkness. "Bloody hell, where's the light switch?"

"It's up by the projection unit at the back," Mary said. "Hang on and I'll get it. I'd use my phone for a light but Lois borrowed it earlier and forgot to give it back." She fumbled her way up the middle of the seats until she got to the back wall. She hit a switch and the ground lighting came on, illuminating the path through, but not the main lights.

"Strange, I lost my phone yesterday," Bright said.

"Perhaps it's our foot fetish thief?" Mary suggested. "Moving on to more profitable things. Although my phone's about three years old and the home button keeps jamming, so they won't get much for it." She made her way down the stairs, feeling weirdly awkward being in the cinema alone with him.

What would it be like if they were on a date? she wondered. Would they sit in the back row? Share popcorn?

"The bloody door's stuck," Bright said, tugging on it.

"It can't be."

"Well, it can, because it is." He was jiggling the handle and leaning his weight into the door, his shoulder against it. "Hello?" he called. "Can anyone hear me?"

"How odd," Mary said. "It's usually left open until the movie begins, hooked back by clips."

"Hello?" Bright yelled, banging his forearms and fists against the padded panel.

"It's soundproof, I think." Mary hoped he wasn't claustrophobic.

"Helpful to know," he muttered, like she was to blame somehow.

"We could ring for help?" she suggested.

He gave her a rather withering look. "On what exactly?"

"Sorry." She'd forgotten neither of them had their phones, but he didn't need to be such an arse. She sat down in one of the seats in the front row, resigned, and watched him pace around the room, looking for a magic exit or telephone to appear. It was a little insulting, how much he seemed to want to get out of there. Maybe it was her?

"You're not claustrophobic, are you?" she asked. He was back at the door, inspecting the handle.

"No. Why? Are you?"

She laughed. "Considering I once went spelunking in

Vietnam, no. I thought you seemed nervous." She motioned to the seat next to her. "Why don't you sit? Someone's bound to come along soon."

He sat down, his long legs stretched out in front of him.

"Spelunking, huh? I guess you've got the body for it." It was hard to tell in the dark, but he seemed like he was embarrassed after he said that. "I mean you're tiny. Mostly. I'm not saying you don't have curves, but proportionally, you know ..." He trailed off and she tried not to laugh.

"Yeah, I guess my mum forgot to feed me one time too often."

He turned to look at her, horror on his face. "Fuck, sorry, I didn't mean ..."

She laughed again. "Relax, I was joking." She gave his leg a pat. His thigh felt very firm under her hand. "Mum and Gran were both small too. Gran wasn't even five feet. She used a step ladder to get into the top cupboards of the kitchen. She'd always say how much she missed Grandad when she got out that ladder."

"Was he tall then?" Bright asked. "Although I suppose he would have seemed tall to her even if he was five foot five." Mary could hear the humour in his voice.

"He was actually about your height. My dad was tall too apparently. Tall and married, according to Gran. I guess we Star women like them taller." As soon as she said it, she felt a bit stupid. Would he think she was hitting on him because of his height? Was she?

"Only Dallas isn't very tall," Bright said. "Not quite married either," he muttered under his breath.

What was up with him and his obsession with Dallas?

"Bright, just to clarify, I'm not dating Dallas, okay?" He looked surprised. Why was he surprised? She'd already told him that at the pool. "Never was, never will," she added firmly.

"Right. Ummm, okay. I'm sorry. I clearly got the wrong end of the stick. I thought when he had your earring that … sorry."

"Yes, I gathered that," she said drily, "when you questioned my morals at the pools."

"God, I'm an idiot," he said.

"You are," she agreed, trying to keep a straight face. Should she say anything more? What the hell. You only live once. "I'm thinking you might have missed the bit where I said I was more interested in you, too?"

She watched his face in the dim light, his eyes rather intense on hers. He leant in towards her and a small shiver went up her back. Was he going to kiss her?

"Was?" he asked, his voice low and husky.

Her breath caught. Please kiss me, she thought.

"I bleeding well told you they were in here." Dougal was pushing on the door, the light sharp as it cut back into the room. They drew apart.

"Gosh, so they are," Lois said, but her voice sounded oddly irritated.

"The popcorn machine's gone mad," Dougal told them. "There's bits everywhere."

THE NEWSIE

Less than a week until Christmas!

Lunch will be at one o'clock, with surprise entertainment to follow.

Don't forget, it's fancy dress!

A reminder that cribbage is being held at the Elms this week. The van will leave here at nine sharp.

Unfortunately, pickleball has had to be cancelled, due to Merv needing a hernia surgery. Games will resume again in the New Year.

The walking club is having a meeting tonight at 7 pm for anyone interested. Discussion will focus on where next year's trip will be. All welcome.

CHAPTER 25

Mary

Jerry stood in front of Mary with an open cookbook pressed to his chest. "I was wondering if I could enlist your help," he said. "Do you think this would be too complicated for a novice? I'm not much of a cook."

The recipe he proffered was for Creamy Chicken with Lemon and Dill sauce and looked to have several steps, any of which could potentially go wrong.

"It looks very fancy."

"I'd like to make a nice meal for Lois." His cheeks turned slightly pink. "To say thank you for all the things she does for me."

"That's a lovely idea, but you don't have to do anything extravagant. I'm sure she'd appreciate whatever you made. And your company, of course."

"That's true, I suppose, but I would like to make something edible. Would you help me?"

"Of course. When were you thinking?"

"I'm going to invite her for tomorrow night, so I can get the ingredients today. If she says yes."

They settled on Chicken Chasseur with baked potatoes and a simple salad. Mary told him it would be easy to make the chicken ahead and that she'd help him assemble it the next afternoon. Then he'd just need to pop it in the oven and put the timer on. Jerry dashed off to see Lois, a little spring in his step.

It should be that simple, she thought. She could invite Bright to dinner and he'd say either yes or no. Her chest fluttered when she thought of the near kiss. Or what she thought was a near kiss. She had wanted him to kiss her. Quite a lot.

If she was completely honest, she wanted more than a kiss. He was her boss though, and that made things tricky. So, until Andrew came back from paternity leave, she'd shelve her thoughts. There would be no dinner invitation.

To distract herself from thoughts of Bright, she picked up the phone and called Larry's Liquor, who confirmed they were able to deliver a Christmas order to the Palms in the morning.

There were eight people waiting for Mary in the reception area for the monthly 'Midday Mavericks' lunch outing. Glenda, who considered herself a 'foodie', had chosen the restaurant, even though she was new to the village. Dale and Sherry always took advantage of the free shuttle, which meant they could 'have a few tipples' and it was usually a lively drive to the restaurant and a very quiet one back again, as most of the passengers snoozed after their lunch.

Mary backed the van around and Bright came out of his office to help the residents embark.

"Why don't you come and eat with us, Mary?" Sherry said. "We have ever so much fun."

"I'm taking the van for its warrant, or I would." Mary slid open the side door. "Then I need to google some entertainment for the Christmas party." She'd tried two alternative magicians, neither of whom would work on Christmas Day.

Dale helped his wife up the ramp to the van. "Sherry and I went to a marvellous wee show at Cork and Fork last week. Wonderful singer. I'm sure she mentioned she was available for private functions."

"Yes, she did." Sherry's eyes lit up. "She was delightfully festive, Mary. Little tassels on her costume. You should go along and see for yourself."

"I've never been there," Mary said. "Did you catch her name? I'm not sure I want to go to a bar alone, but I might give them a call and see if they'll pass on her number."

Bright cleared his throat. "If you wanted, I could go with you. As a work colleague, of course. It might be best to check her out before you hire her."

"Would you?" Mary's heart gave a little skitter at the thought of spending the evening with him. Even if it was work related. "You're right, it would be a good idea to see her perform in person."

"Tomorrow night? I could pick you up at around seven, if that suits."

Mary put on what she hoped was her professional face. "Yes, that sounds fine." Then she totally ruined the professionalism. "I'll be there with bells on."

Bright grinned. "The sparkly earrings should be enough."

She helped Francine and Bets find seats and hauled herself inelegantly up into the driver's seat. One of the perils of being so short. As she pulled the door closed, she noticed Bright watching, his smile even wider.

The line was surprisingly short and the van passed its warrant with flying colours. Mary's regular hairdresser was nearby so she popped in to make an appointment, not feeling too hopeful at such a busy time of year.

"I could fit you in now, if you only want a re-dye," Sierra told her, touching the ends of Mary's hair. "I had a cancellation. Your cut is holding out pretty well. Same colour? Or I have a lovely deep violet that would look stunning with your eyes."

It took even longer to get everyone back into the van as they were all a little tipsy. Except for Glenda, who seemed a bit put out. "I was absolutely mortified," she told Mary, eyeballing Dale and Sherry who were giggling and leaning on each other in the back. "No decorum."

"We had a Slow Comfortable Screw and then Sherry had two Slippery Nipples," Dale slurred.

"I had an Espresso Martini," Bets chimed in. "I'll hardly sleep tonight. Your hair looks lovely, Mary, like a beautiful pixie."

Cocktails. Mary breathed a sigh of relief. There would be no need to expect a call from the restaurant for indecent exposure or inappropriate behaviour.

"The food was wonderful. Well done, Glenda, maybe you should choose again next time," Sherry offered. Glenda stopped scowling.

Within minutes, heads were nodding and there was a chorus of gentle snores from the back.

It was a lovely, sunny afternoon and after three by the time they arrived back at the Palms. Mary decided she'd get everyone sorted and go home early. She could work just as easily at home and she had a bit of a headache.

Klaus was in the lobby as everyone unloaded. "Did I miss lunch?" he asked. He sounded disappointed.

Bets peered at him. Her glasses were sitting wonkily on top of her head. "You're not dressed for it anyway," she said. "Why are you wearing your pyjamas?"

"Am I?" He glanced down at himself.

"Yes, but that red is very nice on you."

CHAPTER 26

Buying all the gifts from the 'Twelve Days of Christmas' song would cost you a fair bit of money. The most expensive being the 'swans a-swimming' which would set you back around $3,000. There would also be 23 birds in total, which means there would be a lot of bird poo.

Bright

It took Bright over an hour to clear the bird shit off the car roof and it still wasn't as perfect as his dad would normally have expected it. He was tugging the car cover over the top of it when Klaus wandered up the drive carrying half a dozen mesh bags, full of oranges.

'What on earth are you going to do with all of those?" Bright asked. "Start up a juice stand at the gate?"

Klaus looked at him like he was a bit simple. "Not everyone can afford fruit, you know," he told Bright as if the answer was obvious. Perhaps he *was* planning a stand? He followed his dad up the drive.

"Shall I put the jug on?" Klaus offered, manoeuvring past a large object in his doorway.

"What the hell?" Bright said, stepping around folded cardboard packaging. "Dad, why do you have a huge throne blocking your doorway?" The chair was massive, the width of two regular chairs, with a tall back covered in red velvet, with gold ornate carvings of vines and berries around the edges and feet. "Where did you get this?"

Klaus put the oranges on the bench and started making tea. Bright wasn't sure if he was purposely ignoring him, or hadn't even registered the chair was there.

"Milk and sugar?" Klaus asked.

He took the packaging from the chair up to the dumpster, folding the cardboard and foam paper to minimise it. As he put down the lid, something brushed up against his leg, making him jump. He may also have let out a little high-pitched squeak, but since no one but the orange cat beside him had heard, he didn't think it counted. Thank God, it's the cat, he thought. Bright did not do well with rodents.

"Hello, buddy," Bright said, reaching down slowly, dangling his fingers and letting the cat get used to him. He gave his head a careful pat. The cat purred and wound himself around Bright's legs. "Did you find your bowl?" Bright asked.

"Come on, let's go fill it up." He started walking slowly towards his office, the cat trailing behind him. "Good boy, you want some nice bikkies, don't you?" he said, aware that he was doing that stupid voice people did with kids and animals.

"Who are you talking to?" Mary said behind him, and he did another jump, and possibly a little squeak, although he thought he might be able to pass that off as the cat. Except the cat had disappeared, he realised.

"Hi, Mary, right, yes … I was actually trying to trap the stray cat that's lurking around. Take it down to the SPCA or something. It's a ratty old thing."

Mary looked horrified. "Bright, you can't take an old cat down there, especially at this time of year. They'll put it down. No one will want to adopt an old cat when it's kitten season. You'd be signing its death warrant."

"Right, no, you're probably right," Bright said, feeling like a jerk. "He's gone again in any case. Your hair looks nice, by the way."

It did. It was a sort of purple colour and he liked it even better than the pink.

"Thanks," Mary said, sounding surprised. "I thought I may as well join all the oldies with their blue rinses."

"Well, you certainly don't look like an old lady," Bright said, then felt a bit embarrassed. "Are we still on for tonight?"

"Yes, I'm looking forward to it." There was a beeping sound from her pocket and she pulled out a pager. "Oh, it's Bets. She likes to check that her emergency alarm is working."

"How often does she do that?"

"Usually once a month or so, but this is the second time since Ada died. I normally call and we chat for a bit once I assess that she doesn't need help, but she's nearby so I might pop in." She put the pager back into her pocket. "I'll see you later then?"

"Yes, okay," he said as she took off across the lawn. She was in a pair of pale-yellow overall shorts, her legs bare. She had a tattoo on her left ankle, but she was walking too fast for him to tell what it was. He was staring at her legs again, he realised, pulling himself together and heading into his office.

After half a dozen calls, he finally managed to get hold of a locksmith who could come later in the week, and arranged to meet him at Klaus's. He was sorting through emails when his phone, which had mysteriously reappeared on his desk after the cinema incident, lit up with a call. It was Bern.

"You won't believe who I ran into," his brother said. "Tiffany Cooper."

"Really? What did she look like?"

"As hot as ever. And she's single. And — you are going to love me for this — I led her your way." Tiffany had been the most popular girl at their high school, mainly due to her gorgeous long blonde hair and ample chest. "She's a physiotherapist now. I bumped into her at the kids' nativity play. She's got an eight-year-old kid, a boy, I think. Anyway, she's broken up with her partner and she's planning to move home, get a job, all that stuff. I said she should contact you to see if you had any work."

"Right, well, we already have a physio, but I'll ask around," Bright said. He could ask Mary if she knew of any jobs, he thought.

"I only said that so she'd come and see you," Bern told him. He had the same tone as Klaus, Bright thought, as if he was a bit thick. "You could ask her out, finally fulfil our teenage fantasies."

"Ah, right, yes. Thanks." For some reason, Bright didn't feel all that hyped up about the idea. He tried to conjure up some enthusiasm. Tiffany had been lovely. Just his type really, but all he could think about was Mary, and that tattoo.

"Well, you don't sound that keen," Bern said. "Are you seeing someone?"

Bright thought about his date tonight. Only it wasn't really a date, was it?

"No?" he said, but it sounded more like a question.

Bern made a snorting sound. "That sounds interesting." There was a crashing noise and then the sound of a kid wailing. "Fudge. Hang on, Bri." Bright could hear a faint crunching sound and then a lot of tears before Bern came back. "Sorry, the bloody Christmas tree has mysteriously fallen over again, I'll have to go." Bright had the urge to tell Bern about Mary and her tree, how they'd decorated it together.

"All right, talk later?" he said instead.

"Yep. By the way," Bern added, "I had the weirdest dream last night — you had a pet elf called Buddy that you were secretly keeping in your pocket."

Bright laughed. "I was probably just happy to see you," he said.

Bern made a gagging noise. "Tell that to Tiffany Cooper," he said.

THE NEWSIE

Sorry for the late notice, but the Scrabble night has been changed from 7 pm to 6 pm, as the Farleys have an appointment early in the morning with the oncologist.

If you lost a pair of false teeth yesterday, Janice has them on her desk.

Does anyone own the ginger cat that has been seen around the main building?

CHAPTER 27

Mary

Patsy had her work van and they spent the morning running around town dropping off parcels to people in need. It was very rewarding, seeing the gratitude most people had for the help, but Mary was conscious of all the things she still needed to do at the Palms as they popped into house after house with their offerings.

"How is it all going with the Grinch?" Patsy asked as they finally drove back to the charity base offices.

"Actually, he's not so bad," Mary said. "He's got a lovely soft side, when you get to know him a bit, and we've been getting on quite well really. We're going out tonight. For work."

"Why are you blushing?" Patsy said, pulling up the drive at the back of the warehouse.

"What? I'm not." Mary covered her cheeks with her hands.

"It's work. Anyway, I doubt I'm his type."

"Sounds like you want to be though?" Patsy said, undoing her seatbelt. "Be careful, Mary. He is your boss after all."

"Only temporarily," Mary said a bit defensively. "After Andrew comes back, he won't really be." Except he owned the place, she reminded herself.

"Still, is it wise?" Patsy gave her shoulder a pat. "These things don't usually end well. In any case, thanks for the help, I owe you one."

"No problem."

"Actually, what are you up to on Christmas Day? We always need help at the centre serving up the meal."

Mary thought about if for a beat. Her first instinct was to say yes, but hadn't she just come to the realisation that she needed to stop doing that?

"Sorry, Patsy, not this year," she said instead.

Mary biked back to the Palms, thinking about what Patsy had said. She was right. It wasn't professional to be thinking of her boss like she was. Besides, she didn't think Bright even saw her that way. It was silly to get her hopes up about anything between them, and she loved her job, she didn't want to jeopardise it. No, she would go out tonight and treat it as strictly business. It was not a date after all. She would focus on work, and stop thinking there was anything between her and Bright.

But maybe she could help Lois and Jerry find romance, she thought, as she made her way over to Jerry's unit. The vacuum cleaner was out and Jerry hummed cheerfully as he opened the door, a bottle of furniture polish in one hand and a cleaning cloth in the other.

"Looking spick and span, Jerry," Mary said, stepping into his neat little sitting room. The units were all very similar; two bedrooms, four different designs, with slightly different configurations, depending on the section orientation. Jerry's house had a small foyer with the living room straight off it. The furniture was modern and neutral and there was a scented candle burning on the sideboard.

"Thank you so much, my dear, for offering to help. I really do appreciate it." Jerry coiled the cord of the vacuum cleaner and wheeled it to a cupboard in the hallway. "I hope I've got everything I need," he called. "I picked up some fancy crackers and a posh cheese. Do you think that will do for a starter?"

"I think that will be perfect."

He came back into the room. "Would you like a glass of something? Wine? Water?"

"Thanks, but no." It was already three and she was thinking about her date — no, arrangement — with Bright later that night. "Shall we get on with the cooking then?"

They settled on a heavy Le Creuset casserole dish for the Chasseur. It looked to Mary like it had never been used. Jerry chopped onions while she crushed the garlic.

"Oh, blast it, I forgot the chicken pieces," he said, poking his head into the refrigerator.

Mary plastered a smile to her face. "Never mind. How about you sauté the onions and garlic, nice and slowly, and I'll pop down to the shops and get some?"

Mary was waylaid by Viv as she was about to leave. "I think the cat in the *Newsie* might belong to the Fosters," she said. "We could go and check now, if you're not busy?" She was, but went along with Viv anyway.

The Fosters' cat, it turned out, had died two years previously, and Carol Foster was happy to show Mary photos and talk about what a treasure he had been. By the time Mary got home it was after six and she barely had time for a quick shower and change before Bright was due to pick her up.

Bright had on white jeans and a moss-green linen shirt. He looked like an Italian model. Mary felt underdressed in her off-the-shoulder summer dress, but when she got in his car, he took a long time taking her in before he told her she looked amazing, so maybe what she had on was fine.

His car smelt like him, woody and fresh, and he had jazz playing softly.

"Have you been to this Cork and Fork place before?" he asked.

"No, I'd never even heard of it, but Sherry said it's been open for about six months."

"Well, let's hope this woman is good. Did you end up getting a name? What sort of entertainment is it? Is she a singer?"

"Her name's Lovey Dixon. Sherry said she sings and dances. I hope she's okay. And not too expensive. I'm running out of options for entertainment."

The place was dimly lit, with a neon sign of a cork pushed onto the tines of the fork hanging above the entrance. A short, tattooed guy in a leather vest sat on a stool by the front door, chewing his thumb nail and scrolling on a phone.

"Ten-dollar cover charge," he said, barely looking up.

"Oh, okay." Mary fumbled in her purse. "Cash? Or do you have a machine?"

"I've got it," Bright told her, handing the guy a twenty.

"Sorry," Mary said, "I thought it was more of a restaurant than a bar." She hoped they had snacks at least. She hadn't eaten.

Inside it was very red. The lighting, the carpet and the booths along the back wall were all a dark shade of burgundy. Most of the tables were full and several waitresses in black dresses, hair slicked back and lips the colour of blood, moved around delivering drinks. A long resin bar inlaid with wine corks ran along one wall, illuminated by wine bottles suspended from the ceiling above it, fairy lights inside the glass. A huge chandelier hung from the centre of the room, made entirely of forks, the tines all bent into scrolls.

"Well, this is funky," Mary said.

A leggy waitress sidled up beside them, smiling broadly. She had a piercing in her lower lip.

"Hi, welcome to Cork and Fork," she said. "I'm Onyx. Table for two?" She was eyeing up Bright as she spoke, like he was a meal.

"Yes, please," Mary said. "We're actually here to watch Lovey, so if we could get a table close to the stage?"

Onyx slid her eyes over to Mary, then up, and down. "All right then. Follow me."

Their table was at the end of one side of the stage. The chairs were angled so they were both facing it.

"Entertainment starts in about fifteen minutes," Onyx said. "Can I get you a drink? Something to eat?" She passed them both a menu. Mary scanned it quickly. There were several food options, thankfully.

"Want to share a bottle of wine?" Bright asked. "Or would you prefer a cocktail?"

"I wouldn't mind a beer, actually."

In the end, they ordered some spring rolls and loaded wedges as well as a craft beer for her and, surprisingly, a cocktail for him. It turned up in a tall glass with a neon flashing base which made her grin.

"I have to admit, this is not quite what I was expecting,"

Bright said.

"The drink? Or the place itself?" Mary asked.

"Both. Still, the company is great." He gave her a slow smile. Bloody hell, he really was a bit lovely, Mary thought, taking a sip of her beer and trying not to burp.

From somewhere backstage, music started, low and earthy. A woman emerged in long black boots, up past her thighs, wearing a man's dinner jacket, a dark red tie around her neck.

She began to sing.

CHAPTER 28

Sixty-five per cent of people like to unwrap or give lingerie as a Christmas gift.

Bright

She was a bit like a magpie, Bright thought. Or that sound on a train when the brakes ground, metal on metal. He and Mary gave each other a look, then, when she grinned and then covered her mouth with her hand, he had to look away to avoid laughing out loud. Mary lifted her beer bottle up to her lips, her shoulders shaking. He took a long sip of his drink. It was surprisingly good, with a nice mix of sweet and sour and the aftertaste of passionfruit.

The woman sang on, hitting some notes with extreme force, while others cracked in the middle. Mary made a strangled sound, then bit into a spring roll and discreetly wiped her eyes with her napkin.

Bright was having a fabulous time.

"Oh, no." Mary put down the rest of her roll. "Please tell me she's not …"

Bright stopped watching Mary and looked up at the stage. Lovey had removed the jacket and he was reminded of Sherry's comment about the tassels.

There were two. One for each nipple.

"Do you think perhaps we've seen enough?" he asked.

They'd tried to leave without anyone noticing after Lovey had produced a banana and started to peel it, but Bright doubted anyone else's eyes had been on them.

They got into his car, neither of them daring to look at each other.

"I am so sorry," she said. "I had no idea."

"No, no, not your fault," he insisted, trying not to laugh. "But I don't think it's quite the vibe we want for a Christmas dinner in a retirement village."

"No, I agree," she said. Her voice was unsteady.

He chanced a glance over at her. She was biting on a knuckle. He tried not to laugh, but let out a snort and she looked up at him, her eyes shining, a grin breaking out on her rather lovely face.

By the time they'd finished laughing, his stomach hurt and Mary's mascara was a bit smudgy. Without thinking he leant across the centre console and wiped his thumb under her eye. They both sat there, looking intently at each other, and he wanted to move his hand to her cheek and draw her closer, kiss her pale-pink lips. Their faces were so close, he could feel her breath on his clavicle, warm and inviting.

"I could really go a burger," Mary said.

They went to Burger King. It was full of teenagers in board shorts and sweaty band T-shirts, milling around filling up their cups with as many varieties of soft drinks as possible and throwing fries at each other across the booths.

"God, I love the barbecue sauce they use on these things," Mary said, biting into her burger with enthusiasm. "I swear they must put crack in it, just the smell of it makes me drool." Bright took a sip of his black coffee and ate a few fries, happy just to watch her.

"What's the weirdest thing you've ever eaten?" he asked. Mary thought about it, swirling her straw around in her frozen Coke.

"Hard to say. I had crocodile in Aussie. Umm, kangaroo too. Oh, no, fried tarantulas. In Cambodia."

Bright pulled a face. "What did they taste like?"

"To be honest, I can't really remember. I was drunk. Sort of like crayfish legs maybe? Not bad. But I threw up later." She grinned. "I think that was the alcohol though, not the spiders."

"Do you plan to travel more?" Bright asked. He was hoping she would say no, he realised. He wanted her to stay so he could get to know her better.

"Not on my own, no." She finished off her burger and wiped her fingers on a napkin. "Maybe with the right person though."

He hoped she meant him.

THE NEWSIE

We have been unable to procure entertainment for Christmas Day. If anyone has any party tricks, please let Mary know, otherwise we will be taking requests for a Christmas playlist.If you lost a pair of false teeth yesterday, Janice has them on her desk.

Hope you've all got your letters in for Santa and all our residents are on the 'nice' list!

Gingerbread house making will be on today at 10 am. Come and join us!

CHAPTER 29

Mary

Klaus appeared in front of Janice's desk and both Janice and Mary looked up from where they'd been discussing Christmas party logistics. Mainly whether they should have a seating plan and how many turkeys they'd need, as well as eating the gingerbread house Mary had made that morning.

"Are there any letters for me?" he asked. He was wearing red pyjamas again — though they looked clean and uncrumpled, so not the same ones as earlier in the week — and his gumboots.

"No, Mr Nicols, why would there be?" Janice said. "Unless it's parcels, your mail is always delivered to your letterbox."

"They might not know where to send them," he said. "People can get very confused."

"Dad." Bright strode into the room and Mary gave him a small smile. The corners of his lips quirked and she thought how lovely he looked when he wasn't frowning. "Have you been gardening?"

"No. Why would you think that?"

"You're wearing gumboots," Bright pointed out. Mary wondered what he made of the pyjamas. "So I'm assuming you've been doing some weeding or something."

"We have gardeners for that, it's part of the levies." Klaus narrowed his eyes. "I hope you're not thinking of cutting the budget."

The door burst open and Bets rushed into the room. She was out of breath and had one hand pressed against her ample bosom. "Come quickly. It's Lois," she said. "She's fainted. In the rec room."

"I'll go," Mary offered.

"I think you'd better both come," Bets panted. "Not you, Janice, you can stay here and hold the fort."

Mary followed Bright with Bets bringing up the rear. She gave herself a second to admire the fit of his pants as they all rushed into the lounge. Lois was lying on her back slightly inside the rec room. There was a cushion from one of the armchairs under her head. A few of the residents had gathered around.

"Make room," Bets cried. "Mary has a first-aid certificate. Lois — Bright and Mary are here. Both of them."

Lois let out a little groan and cracked open an eye. Bright hovered nervously and Mary bent to feel her pulse. It was beating steadily, perhaps a little fast. "Can you hear me, Lois? It's Mary," she said.

Lois let out a little sigh and opened both eyes. "Mary, dear."

"Should we call an ambulance?" Bright asked.

"Oh, no, that won't be necessary." Lois sat up rather hastily. "I think it was the heat. Perhaps some water, Bets?"

"I'll get it," Bright said.

"No, no, Bets doesn't mind, do you, Bets?"

"Not at all. I'll just …" Bets gasped dramatically. "Oh, my saints, look at that."

All eyes followed her pointed finger to the mistletoe hanging above the doorway. "Do you know what that means?"

"Why, look at that," Lois gasped. "Mary, you and Bright are standing right underneath."

"Ooh, a mistletoe kiss," Viv said, from nearby.

"I … um … now is hardly the time …" Bright stuttered. "Lois, we need to get someone to check that you're …"

"I'm right as rain," Lois insisted. "But I'll feel much better with a wee Christmas kiss."

Bright looked startled and Mary coughed, to cover a giggle.

"Well, now, I wouldn't want to cause you …"

"Oh, not me, silly man," Lois said. "I mean Mary. You're both right under the doorway. Help me up, Bets, so I can bear witness."

Mary thought Bright was going to object again. His face had turned rather pink. The residents stood, watching them expectantly.

"I think …" Bright started.

Mary wanted badly to kiss him. "It *is* tradition," she said. She leant towards him and went up on her tiptoes. Bright looked momentarily surprised, like a deer in the headlights. Then he stooped and placed one of his big hands on the side of her face. She resisted closing her eyes as his lips gently brushed hers. Mary heard a popping sound, and for a moment she thought it had come from inside of her head. Like the earth had literally moved.

Bright moved away and the kiss was over.

"The lights have blown," Bets said. "How strange."

Mary found it took her a beat to adjust back to reality. It was barely a kiss, but the butterflies were thrashing about inside her chest.

Bets was right. The central chandelier had been on in the living room, as well as the main light in the rec room. The bulbs were now a smoky grey.

"Well, um, that's ... I'll go and get maintenance if you're sure you're all right, Lois? ... See if they've got some spare bulbs," Bright muttered.

"All fine and dandy," Lois said cheerfully. She was looking rather smug.

CHAPTER 30

*There is a village in Peru where, around Christmas time,
people settle the previous year's grudges by fist fighting.
They then start the new year off with a clean slate.*

Bright

"You did it on purpose," Glenda said just as Bright returned with the box of bulbs. She, Dallas and his dad — Glenda's son — had turned up and the small group were all gathered around, Lois and Glenda in the middle of everything, looking frosty. "You knew Dallas and Mary were an item and you couldn't bear the thought that I might get to have her as my daughter-in-law."

"Rubbish," Lois said. "It was a coincidence, and I would have thought you might have a little more concern over the fact that I fainted ..." She picked up a plate off one of the card tables. "In fact, it was probably your baking that did it."

Glenda clutched at her throat. "What on the earth are you saying?" Her eyes widened rather dramatically. "Are you implying I *poisoned* you?"

"Now, ladies," said Jerry stepping in between them, "let's not say anything we might regret."

"Perhaps a nice cup of tea?" Mary suggested.

Klaus took a piece of shortbread off the plate Lois was still holding and bit into it.

"Tastes fine to me," he said. He sat down in a chair to finish it, pulling a notebook out of his pocket and resting it on his belly to make a note with a pencil tucked in behind his ear and mostly obscured by the mop of grey hair he was now sporting.

"Don't go putting words in my mouth," Lois said, thrusting the plate at Glenda rather forcefully. "I was merely saying that these are excessively sweet for my taste. That much sugar could have been the reason I fainted."

"Well, I never." Glenda's voice was dangerously low. "I've never been so insulted in my life." Her fists curled by her side.

Was it his imagination, or were Lois and Glenda squaring off to have an actual punch-up? It felt like everyone might start chanting 'Fight! Fight! Fight!' any minute. A little part of Bright's brain wondered who would win.

"Look, this all seems a bit much over a harmless kiss," he said. Even though it had been rather more than that for him. If all the residents hadn't been there, it felt like it might have been a *lot* more.

"Nan, this is nuts," Dallas said. "Mary and I barely know each other." He turned to look at Mary. "Not that you're not very nice, you are," he smiled.

"Likewise," she said. Bright could feel a growl running up the back of his throat.

"But in any case, I'm with Akira. If Mary and Bright want to kiss, it's nothing for you to worry about."

"It's about more than the kiss," Glenda insisted. "Lois has been rude to me since I got here."

"Only because you're after her man," Bets said. There was an uncomfortable silence. Jerry looked mortified, Glenda and Lois were still glaring, and everyone else had become very interested in the artwork around the room. Several people sidled out, Bets included. Klaus was still jotting things down in his notebook. All the shortbread was gone.

"It shouldn't take more than half an hour," the locksmith had assured him, so Bright was hovering around outside Klaus's house, both to wait for the guy to be done, and half keeping an eye out to make sure Klaus didn't come home and catch him. It was like being a teenager again, keeping watch while Bern siphoned the top off all his dad's booze.

He wasn't really doing anything wrong — if the key to the garage was lost, it needed to be recut, but he still felt a little guilty, like he was invading Klaus's territory or privacy or something.

The cat was back. He clawed insistently at Bright's pant leg until Bright crouched down and gave him a pat, then rolled onto his belly and started to purr. He was a bit of a smooch for such a battle-worn tom.

"All right then, Buddy," Bright crooned. "I'll give you a rub. Look at that belly, you handsome man, all fluffy and ginger."

There was a dry cough and then Mary arrived around the corner of the house. She was making quite a lot of noise for her.

"Bright, I wanted to apologise. For the kiss." She had on cute Christmas pudding earrings and her amethyst hair matched her nail polish. "I didn't mean to force you into it, is what I'm trying to say."

Bright leant down a little, getting closer to her. She smelt like vanilla. "Mary," he said. "There is absolutely no need to apologise to me."

"Yes, but I got the feeling you didn't want to …"

"Oh, I wanted to," he told her firmly. "I absolutely wanted to."

"Oh," she said with a little exhale of breath. "Oh, well, good."

"In fact, I would very much like to …" Bright started to say.

"All done, mate," the locksmith said, poking his head out the ranch slider. Bright pulled reluctantly away from Mary. She was standing with her chin tilted up, eyes wide, and he couldn't remember any more why he had thought she wasn't his type.

"Hope you're not expecting to find any dead bodies in there," the locksmith joked. "If you can't find the key, let me know and I'll come back and replace the whole lock."

Bright watched him get into his car, then turned to Mary. She'd moved away slightly and he felt like he'd imagined the moment they'd had before they were interrupted.

"I don't know why I'm nervous to go inside," he said, picking at the skin on his thumb nail. "It's not like I am actually going to find a dead body inside the garage."

"No missing residents that I know of, so that's a start," Mary said. "Doesn't Klaus know you were having the door unlocked?"

Bright looked down at his feet sheepishly. "He's been cagey about things. Keeps telling me he can't find the key, but I'm sure he's got it. I guess I'm curious to see why he doesn't want me in there. And I need to put the bloody car away."

Mary's eyes sparkled. He hadn't really noticed before what a striking shade of blue they were. "Do you want me to stand guard?" she stage-whispered.

Bright chuckled. "Would you?"

"I'll give you a whistle if I see anything."

He let himself into the garage through the internal door. It was dim and cool inside and he flipped a switch. The fluorescent light flickered on. Boxes were neatly stacked along one wall. The workbench was covered in scraps of wood and sawdust. To one side was a pile of wooden toys — figurines of little people painted bright colours and animals shiny with linseed oil. There was a trestle table covered in wrapping paper, ribbons and scissors. A large tape dispenser sat on one end. Most curious of all was the large, half-built sled in the middle of the garage. Next to it was a large hessian sack of coal.

Some of the stacked boxes had been opened, and Bright lifted a flap and looked inside.

"Holy crap," he said.

Mary must have heard him from outside. "Bright? Is everything okay in there?"

"Hang on." He pressed the opener on the wall and the roller door slid slowly up, revealing first Mary's feet, then her shapely bare legs and, finally, all of her.

"Have a look at this," he said.

They both peered into the box. Mary's eyes grew wide. "Um ... why does your dad have a box full of fluffy handcuffs?"

"I can't think of one single good reason."

Hands on hips, Mary stood and swivelled, taking in the entire space.

"Secret present wrapping?" she asked. "There are enough handcuffs in there for each person in the village."

"That's the thing. Dad doesn't do presents. Not even for me and Bern."

Mary poked her foot at one of the other boxes. "Do you think we should have a look at these?"

"Should we?"

"Most of them have been opened anyway." They looked at each other. Mary lifted the flap to another box and gasped. "Oh, um …" She turned a cute shade of pink. "It looks like a box full of … toys."

"Toys? Maybe for Bern's kids."

"Yeah, not that kind of toy." She opened another carton. Four of them contained assorted sex toys. Thankfully, the next one was full of small packets of chocolates and another held candy canes and bubble blowers.

"Do you think Dad's been targeted by scammers?" Bright asked. He was reluctant to look any more.

There was a sound in the doorway. "What in the blazes are you two doing?"

Klaus looked angrier than Bright had ever seen him. Aside from the time Bern had taken the car out without asking and crashed into the neighbour's fence.

He looked like a wild man, with his shaggy hair and long grey beard. "Shut the bloody door before everyone sees."

"I don't understand, Dad. What are you doing with all this … stuff? Do you even know what these are?" Bright waved a hand at the lurid handcuffs.

"Of course I bloody do," Klaus said. "The one-day sale said toys were fifty per cent off. I thought there would be a bit more variety, but I guess children still like to play cops and robbers, don't they?"

Mary cleared her throat. "These aren't toys for kids, Klaus."

"Why would you buy so many toys? Are these all for Bern's

kids?" Bright asked.

"They're for all of the children," Klaus said belligerently. "Well, all the good ones."

Bright felt an uncomfortable prickling of realisation. "What do you mean, Dad?"

His father was looking at him like he thought Bright was stupid. "Well, the cat's out of the bag now, isn't it? I suppose you're old enough to know the truth. In fact, I could probably do with a couple of helpers."

Beside him, Mary let out a choked noise.

"You have to promise not to spoil the secret. If everyone knew where Santa Claus lived, I'd never get any peace."

"Dad, you're not actually ..."

"Of course we'll help." Mary gave Bright a look.

"Good. Can you sew? Because I'm having trouble with this blimmin' machine."

Klaus had brought his office chair from inside and set it up next to the old sewing machine in a corner of the garage. There was a colourful pile of fabric and a few reels of coloured ribbon on the table next to it.

"Actually, I'm an excellent seamstress," Mary said as she wandered over for a closer look. She picked up a spotty knee-high sock from the pile and held it aloft.

"Bright, I think we might have solved the mystery of the sock thief."

CHAPTER 31

According to tradition, you should eat one mince pie on each of the 12 days of Christmas to bring good luck. However, it's technically illegal to eat mince pies on Christmas Day in England. In the 17th century, Oliver Cromwell banned Christmas pudding, mince pies and anything to do with gluttony. The law has never been rescinded.

Bright

"I think Dad's lost it," Bright said, pacing back and forth in his office. "Like really lost his marbles, Bern."

"I don't get what you mean," his brother said. "So he thinks he's Santa? For real?"

"It all makes sense now," Bright said. "All the gumboots and red pyjamas and not wanting to cut his hair." Bright picked up the cat and sat down, settling Buddy on his lap.

"Mary says I should just let him think it. But why? Why does he think he's bloody Santa?"

"I've no idea," Bern said. "But it is a bit of a worry. Wait, who's Mary?"

"She's ..." Bright had the stupid urge to say something like 'the woman I'm going to marry' or at least 'the woman I think I might be in love with'. "... she's our activities coordinator," he said instead. Which really didn't seem enough.

"Right, well, she might have a point," Bern said. "It's only a couple of days until Christmas, so maybe we should play along? It's not like we can do anything at this time of year anyway, can we?"

"I suppose not," Bright said doubtfully. "But honestly, Bern, the boxes of sex toys, and the stealing of people's socks, and he's deliberately putting on weight, I think. We should have invested shares in mince tarts."

"Or vibrators," Bern said, making Bright laugh.

"Dad? What's a bibrator?" Lucy asked, and Bright cracked up.

"I'd better leave you to it," he said.

"Thanks, mate," Bern said drily. "I am sorry that I'm not there to help though. I wish there was something more helpful I could say."

"We'll work it out." He hung up. Buddy was contentedly purring on his lap so he sat there for a while, stroking his soft fur and thinking. Was all this Santa stuff something to do with his mum? With the video he'd found on his dad's

TV? He thought about Mary and her love for Christmas. How would he feel if she was gone? Would he want to shut out Christmas altogether? Or keep it alive for her?

"I'll play the ivories," Dougal said, interrupting his thoughts. He was standing in the doorway, his back a bit stooped, permanent frown lines on his forehead.

I'll end up like him, Bright thought, if I keep being such a Grinch.

"Did you hear me? I said I'll play the piano. On Christmas Day."

Bright wondered if could even play. Perhaps he was like Klaus and had decided he was a concert pianist. But they didn't have anything else lined up.

"Thank you, Dougal, that sounds … most helpful."

"I *can* play," Dougal said, perhaps hearing the hesitation in Bright's voice. "Haven't done it for a few years, but it's like riding a bike, isn't it?"

Bright tried to imagine Dougal on a ten-speed and failed. A penny-farthing maybe? "I'm sure it will be wonderful," he said. "And I appreciate your offering to help."

Dougal shuffled a bit in his slippers. "Well, I might have been a bit rude to that Mary, in hindsight," he said. "Bad time of year."

"I know what you mean," Bright said. "But Mary is very forgiving. And I'm sorry for your loss."

Dougal just nodded and left. He was going to make sure he didn't become a bitter old man, Bright decided. Starting now.

Dallas pulled up by the front entrance and Bright helped him unload the music equipment and cart it into the main lounge where they planned to set up for the party.

"Thank you so much for doing this," Bright told him. "We really appreciate it."

"No worries, mate," Dallas said, "happy to help. I'm sorry I can't do the music on the day, but we have to be at Akira's folks for lunch and they're an hour away, so …"

"No, no. This is great." Bright cleared his throat. "Listen, Dallas, I'm sorry if I've been a bit of a jerk to you. I think maybe I got the wrong end of the stick over you and Mary and …"

"Honestly, mate, I hadn't noticed," Dallas said.

Shit, maybe he'd only thought to himself that Dallas was a cheating jerk? Had he never said anything to Dallas?

"Hello, Dallas," Mary said, coming through from the side door. "Thought I heard your voice."

"Just dropping off the deejay gear," Dallas said, arranging the deck and speakers on a table.

"I hope you'll get a chance to join us for the Christmas party," Mary said. "I'm keen to reconnect with Akira."

"Yeah, we might pop in on our way, if that's all right? Have a drink with Nan." He looked at his phone. "Crap, I have to get going. I'm supposed to be picking Akira up."

He gave them a wave and left Bright and Mary standing in

the lounge looking at each other.

"I was thinking ..." Bright said, a bit distracted. It was an elf, he realised. On her ankle. A cute little cartoon elf with pointy ears and bells on its shoes. He couldn't stop looking at it. Or at her legs which seemed much longer up close and ...

"I don't want to rush you," Mary said, but I do have meditation class in ten minutes."

"Right, yes." Bright tried to think what he had been planning to say. "Right, umm, I was thinking. About the boxes in Dad's garage."

"Okay?"

"I wondered if any of them might be of use, for the party?" he asked. "Not the sex stuff, obviously." He felt the heat rising up his neck. "But the food or any of the other stuff really."

Mary looked excited. "Oh, yes, that could be good. I noticed there were some cute snowglobes we could use on the tables, and I'm sure we can repurpose some of the other things." This time it was her that looked a bit embarrassed. "Maybe not the rude ones ... But thanks."

"My pleasure," he said. "Let me know if you want some help with it." He headed out the door, then changed his mind and went back. "Actually, Mary, I was wondering if you were free tomorrow?"

THE NEWSIE

A reminder that the Christmas party is dress-up. So dig out your fun and festive costumes! There will be a prize for the best dressed.

If you have signed up for the pet-feeding service over Christmas, please take in any instructions and food to the office by 5 pm today.

It's nearly Christmas, folks!!

CHAPTER 32

Mary

Bright had asked her out on a date. All morning as she did the last-minute party organising, she thought about it. He hadn't said where he was taking her, just that she didn't need to get dressed up.

Andrew was back in the New Year. Then Bright would go back to his business and she might not see him much. But also that would mean he wasn't her 'boss' as such. This would be good because what Mary wanted to do with Bright was not something you should do with your boss.

The area beside the bar was the biggest space in the communal rooms, so Mary had set up the tables in there, dragging in the chairs they used for events and stacking all the plates, cutlery and tablecloths in a tidy pile of boxes and crates ready to be laid out tomorrow. She was getting excited for Christmas now, she thought as she surveyed the room.

The tree looked lovely, even with the cheap paper chains,

and the room was decorated, the music sorted. She hoped Dougal was okay on the piano. It was a lovely black baby grand and she didn't want him banging away and ruining it somehow.

The shopping was put away in the kitchen. Jars of cranberry sauce and mustard in the cupboard, cream and custard in the fridge. Mary ticked off a pile of things on her list, feeling satisfied. All she had left to do was chill the wine, brine the turkeys and prepare the potatoes, then on Christmas Day she would cook those, decorate the pavlovas and dress the salads. It was a shame the budget hadn't stretched to something a bit more exciting, but she was happy enough now everything was done.

She'd found a lot of useful things in Klaus's garage, even a few bottles of alcohol. After checking with Bright, she'd used some to make brandy butter and put the others behind the bar.

Last night she had done a bit of sewing and decorated some of the socks with ribbon and edging. She thought they had turned out quite well, with little bottles of bubbles, mini fans, oranges, nuts and chocolates stuffed inside them. There were forty-five residents coming and she had made one for each of them. She made a mental note to bring them up in the morning.

Mary had almost finished her costume for the party too and she had a bag of fun headbands and hats for those residents who didn't want to dress up. She stacked those and the other plastic container full of homemade Christmas crackers onto the box of table decorations and then headed out to meet Bright.

He was standing outside next to his car, talking to Klaus who was eating yet another Christmas mince pie. There were still three boxes of them in the garage.

"I thought you could take me to the mall," Klaus said.

"Absolutely not," Bright said firmly.

"All right but in that case, I'll need your help bringing my chair up to the clubhouse," Klaus told him. "You can do it tomorrow."

Bright sighed, then smiled when he caught Mary's eye. "I'll see you later, Dad. Mary and I are off on a date." He opened the passenger door for her. "Ready?"

"That cat seems to have found you," Mary commented as they drove. Bright looked over at her briefly, then back at the road.

"What? Buddy? No, I mean he's not mine," Bright said, then paused. He gave her a funny look. "Do you know what? You might be right. Bloody hell. I have a cat."

"Or he has you."

They drove into town, past the shops that were busier than usual with all the pre-Christmas rush. All the shops' displays were Christmas themed, some with fake snow borders. Most of the awnings and doorways were decorated and the trees lining the street had lights or baubles on them. It looked beautiful. Mary sighed contentedly.

"Doesn't everything look so amazing at this time of year? I love Christmas."

"Well, I hope you'll like this then." Bright pulled into a car park and looked for a spot. Mary could see a large archway a little way down the path, with a line of fake trees, covered in white snow. Lights hung from the arch and two giant blow-up candy canes sat either side of the entrance.

"Oh, my goodness, what is this?" she asked, bouncing a little in her seat. Bright had spotted a people mover backing out and he indicated to go in, manoeuvring his car back into the park in that way some people make look so easy and cool.

"I saw it advertised. Come on."

They got out and lined up behind a woman with a push-chair and two small kids. Mary could smell candy floss and there was a gorgeous blue vintage caravan parked out front selling hot chocolate. A large hanging sign read 'CHRIST-MAS ON ICE'.

"I hope you can skate?" Bright said.

He'd taken her to a Winter Wonderland. A Christmas-themed skating rink. It was the most romantic thing that had ever happened to her and Mary thought she might burst with joy.

"Just so you know," she said, "this is the best date I've ever been on."

CHAPTER 33

*In the UK, for a Christmas to be officially classified as
'white', a single snowflake needs to be observed falling in
the 24 hours of the 25th of December on the rooftop of
the Met Office HQ in London.*

Bright

The guy selling the entry tickets was very short, wearing a
pair of reindeer antlers and a red nose. He looked like he
would rather be anywhere than behind a makeshift desk at
a skating rink. There was a large machine that looked like
a leaf blower on the counter that he had to keep peering
around.

"Sorry 'bout the snow machine," he said. "It's for sale if
you want to buy it?"

"Yeah, no," Bright declined. "Just the skating, thanks."

"What size boots do you need?" the guy asked after Bright

had paid, pointing at a shelf to their left lined with ice skates. Bright had to repress a shudder. It was like putting on bowling shoes. The thought made his skin crawl. But Mary was quite literally bouncing up and down with excitement, so he took a pair of skates and they went through the gate.

"Oh, man, sorry. It's not as big as it looked in the photos," he told Mary, taking in the rink. It was not much bigger than a backyard swimming pool and crawling with children pushing penguin aids to help them along the ice. He'd been hoping for something a bit more romantic, like in the movies. This one had several giant blow-up snowmen and one giant Santa that looked like he had a slow leak, his face hunched into his neck like he was asleep. The ubiquitous Christmas carols playing on a scratchy speaker couldn't hide the drone of the motors.

"It never is," Mary said with a grin. "No, seriously, Bright, it's amazing." She led him over to a tiered seat to change into their skates. "I love ice skating."

Bright had only been once before as a kid, but he put on his skates feeling fairly confident he would do fine. A kid in a full ski outfit whizzed past them, making it look easy.

"Oh, here." Bright reached into his pocket and pulled out the purple gloves he'd bought. "You might want these."

Mary's face lit up. It was like he'd given her jewellery. She rubbed the angora wool against her face and sighed.

"Thank you, they're gorgeous. I'm so excited." She stood and made her way over to the barrier, balancing easily on her boots, and glided out onto the ice, doing a little swirl and then came back to rest against the side, waiting for him.

It was quite tricky, walking on the thin blades, Bright thought, but it would be much easier once he was on the ice. He made it to the edge and then stepped out gingerly, gripping onto the railing, his feet sliding precariously.

"Do you need a walker?" Mary asked, skating backwards and circling back around to him.

"No," Bright said, but he kept one hand firmly on the rail as he attempted to move. "No, I'll be fine, just a little rusty. You go ahead while I get my bearings."

Mary gave him another huge grin and skated off to do a loop of the rink. He watched her briefly, dodging easily around the other skaters, but then he wobbled again and almost lost his footing. Concentrating hard (how difficult could it be to move one foot in front of the other?) he let go of the rail and shuffled slowly forward. Mary skated back to him, cheeks pink and eyes shiny.

"You're doing great." She spun backwards in front of him and held out both hands. "Here. We'll take it slowly."

There was some innuendo in there, Bright thought, but he tentatively reached out and felt her firm grip. For someone so tiny, she was strong and solid. They made it all the way around, and then Mary released one hand and they did another circle side by side. They crawled along and he flailed about but Mary adjusted her pace to his.

"Sorry I'm so slow," he said.

"I don't mind. I'm having the best time." Two small girls, giggling, passed them. "Here, try this," Mary said. "Keep your feet about shoulder-width apart and your shoulders back." She demonstrated and Bright copied. "Now keep your weight on the back half of the skates. Better?"

It was. He felt less like a gormless giraffe. They skated, Mary humming along to 'Joy to the World'.

"Do you want me to let go of your hand now?"

"Never," Bright said. But she let his hand go. He looked over at her and had the thought that he'd like to do this again sometime, but in winter, on a proper rink, with real snow and sleigh bells …

Something smashed into the back of his legs and he felt himself lurch. He almost managed to steady himself again. Then he teetered, his feet shot out in front of him and he crashed to the ground. The kid with the penguin skater who had collided with him charged on obliviously.

"Bright, are you okay?" Mary held out a hand and pulled him to his feet.

"Yeah, I'm good." He was going to have a massive bruise on his arse the next morning and his knee was a bit sore.

"Do you want to stop? There's a coffee stand, if you want to sit down."

"Nah, let's keep going. I felt like I was finally getting into my stride." He really wasn't, but he didn't want to stop. He didn't want to spoil her fun. And she might hold his hand again.

Mary laughed and reached out her hand. "You were improving," she said. "Not sure about getting into your stride, but we've still got a few minutes left for you to show me your stuff."

The kid who had crashed into Bright had stopped in front of them, hunched over his walker. Mary started to guide them around him when there was a gagging sound and the kid projectile vomited, a stream of sticky blue spreading across the white ice.

The bell rang to end the session. "Everyone off the ice. Please make your way to the entrance."

The warm fug of the air outside was jarring after the chill of the ice rink. Mary pulled off her gloves. They were the same colour as her hair and Bright wondered whether he'd realised that when he bought them.

"Shall we get hot chocolate?" she asked.

He took her hand and pulled her to the side so that they were concealed between a fake Christmas tree and a blow-up snowman. "What would you say if I told you we were standing under some mistletoe right now?"

Mary glanced up. They weren't. For a second she looked confused but then she smiled. "I'd say you should kiss me."

So he did. This time without an audience he kissed her properly. Her lips were warm and soft and she brought her hands up and placed them solidly against his back. He could feel them against his T-shirt and pulled her closer. When he paused for a breath, she kissed him again.

"That day under the mistletoe?" he said, his voice a little hoarse. "This is what I really wanted to do."

"If you had, Lois would have fainted for real."

"Do you think she was faking it?"

Mary snorted. "She was definitely faking it. That was a miraculous recovery."

"Wait a minute. Do you think she locked us in the cinema too?"

"And took our phones."

"Well, that would explain the weird pat she gave my bum."

"Well, it is a very nice bum. Hopefully not too bruised after hitting the ice." She stepped closer towards him. "Damn Dougal opening that door too soon."

Bright cleared his throat. "I don't want to be presumptuous, and we can get hot chocolate here if you'd rather. But I made some eggnog and I was wondering ... would you like to come back to my place?"

"I'd love to go back to yours for eggnog," Mary said. "We might even get round to drinking it."

Bright choked out a laugh. He kissed her again and then took her hand and they speed-walked back to the car.

Bright fumbled with the key to his house, not wanting to let go of Mary's hand. They had been leaning against the door and, when he managed to get it open, they stumbled inside. He wanted to kiss Mary against the wall, to pick her up and cup her bum while he carried her upstairs …

"Surprise. Sorry, mate, I hope you don't mind that we let ourselves in."

"Uncle Bright, we've been waiting for you for *ages*."

Bright noticed the suitcases in the foyer. Bern, Di and the kids stared back from where they sat, in a row, on his sofa.

CHAPTER 34

In 1826, eggnog caused a riot at the West Point military academy Christmas party when, despite a no-alcohol policy, cadets partied with the spiked drink. The festivities led to two assaults and the destruction of the barracks. Dozens of cadets were brought up on charges and suspended.

Mary

The man on the sofa looked eerily like Bright. Almost a carbon copy, except, to Mary, he was lacking something. Despite him being a smilier version, she preferred Bright's more serious face. His dark hair was slightly flecked with grey, cut in a very similar style, and his long legs sprawled out in front of him. The little girl who had been sitting on his knee leapt up and launched herself at Bright.

"Luce." Bright bent to put an arm around her and lift her.

She wrapped her legs around him like a crab. His other hand still held Mary's in a firm grip.

"We've been here for ages and Mummy said I wasn't allowed to eat any of your food and all I've had is a glass of water."

"Lucy, mind your manners," the woman said. "Hi, Bri, sorry to spring this on you. It was a bit of a last-minute thing and we thought it would be nice to surprise you." She came over for a hug and glanced down at their joined hands. "And sorry, this is?"

"Sorry, Di, this is Mary. Mary, my sister-in-law Diane — and that's my brother Bern and Lucy and Tate."

"Mary?" Bern barked out a huge laugh. "As in activities coordinator Mary?"

What had Bright said about her? She was surprised he'd even mentioned her, but for some reason it made her heart do a little skip.

"There's chocolate stoorberries in the fridge," Lucy said hopefully. "They're a bit messy looking. Mummy is much better at them."

Bright chuckled. "Yeah, you guys can have them."

Lucy wriggled out of Bright's grasp and she and Tate scuttled over to the fridge.

"Hang on, I'll help," Di said, going over to assist.

Had he made them for her? Bright gave Mary's hand a squeeze and then he let it go and went to embrace his brother. She felt the loss like a missing glove.

"Great to see you, man, I'm so glad you're here."

"Yeah, after we talked I said to Di that I was worried about Dad and she suggested we get on a flight and go." Bern looked over at Mary and smiled. Then frowned. "Oh sh— darn. Did we interrupt something? Sorry."

"No, no, you're fine," Mary said, "but maybe I should go and let you guys catch up?"

"No, stay," Bright said. "Please."

"Yes, stay," Bern agreed. "We can get some takeaways, crack open one of Bright's wines from his stash, and get acquainted."

"If you're sure?"

Di called out from where she had the kids set up at Bright's table, paper towels tucked into their collars. The strawberries were almost all gone, except for the bits all over Lucy and Tate's faces. "Yes, please stay, Mary. Bright, what's the stuff in the yellow jug in the fridge? If I didn't know you better I'd have said it was eggnog?"

"It is actually," Bight said, looking a bit embarrassed.

"Right, shall we try that then," Di suggested. She poured them all a glass and they sat at the table.

Mary glanced around the house, feeling a bit curious. It wasn't what she would have expected. The furniture looked as if it had all come from the same store and Bright had walked in and said 'I'll take that entire display, please.'

"Cheers," Di said, clinking her glass with Mary's.

"Are you a mermaid?" Tate asked around a mouthful of

fruit.

"She's not, because she doesn't have a tail," Lucy told him. "She's a fairy."

"I take it you haven't seen Dad yet?" Bright asked. Bern took a sip of his drink and then pulled a face.

"Nah, we thought we'd go in the morning? Have you got any beer?"

The eggnog was a bit odd, Mary had to admit. A bit thick and weird tasting. Bern had gone over to the fridge and she wondered how rude it would be to ask him to get her a beer too. Bern caught her looking and lifted his bottle, eyebrow raised in a question. She nodded and he grinned, coming back to the table with four bottles.

"Sorry, Bri, but that stuff is hideous." He handed Bright a beer. "So, is it all good if we stay here?"

Bright glanced over at her, then mouthed 'Sorry'. "Yeah, all good, man," he said.

Mary had a brief pang of regret at what could have been if they'd got back and the house had been empty. They'd have been upstairs right now and ... oh, God, she wasn't even wearing her good underwear. So that was a silver lining, she guessed.

In the end they decided to cook, so while Bright and Bern stood out on the deck talking coal versus gas barbecues and the sausages thawed, Mary and Di rifled through Bright's kitchen for things to go with them, while the kids watched cartoons in the lounge.

Di was an environmental engineer which had intimidated Mary initially but the more they talked, the more they discovered they had in common. Di was a keen cyclist and gardener and they both loved old movies. Di also loved Christmas.

"When I first started going out with Bern, he was hopeless at Christmas stuff." She passed Mary some potato salad dressing and a can of beetroot from the pantry. "He never got me a gift, or wanted to do anything festive, but over the years I've managed to de-Grinch him. Especially since we had the kids." She found an onion and a bag of potatoes and passed them up too. "I think he likes it as much as they do now."

"What do you think about the whole thing with Klaus?" Mary asked, pulling out a pot.

"To be honest I think they should leave him to it. He might not even know what Christmas is in a year or two, and he's not doing any harm, is he? Well, apart from nicking people's socks."

Mary salted the potatoes and turned on the gas. "Did you know the boys when their mum was alive?"

"Only vaguely. I was at the same school, but we didn't really run in the same circles until our final year when one of my girlfriends dated a friend of theirs."

"Are they still together?" Mary asked, topping up their

wine. It was a nice one that Di had picked from what turned out to be an impressive selection in Bright's garage.

"God, no," Di laughed. "No. He cheated on her with the school's hot girl, Tiffany Cooper. Then tried to crawl back to her after when Tiffany told everyone he was a dud in bed."

"Who's a dud in bed?" Bern asked, coming in the door. He pinched Di's bum. "You'd better not be talking about me." Di laughed and gave him a shove.

"Do you really think I'd have stuck around all these years if you weren't a stud in the sack, babe?"

Mary's mind went down a weird path, wondering if twins were identical in all ways, then forced herself to stop thinking about Bright and sex.

The kids were hyper since it felt hours earlier for them, so after dinner they wanted to play games and be piggy-backed and build forts with Bright's cushions. Mary watched him, seemingly unfazed by the chaos and the clambering for his attention. He'd probably make a good dad, she thought. If he wanted them. She did. But they'd only kissed. It was far too early to be imagining herself ten years down the track, married with kids.

"How many sleeps until Christmas?" Lucy asked Bern.

"Two. Tomorrow we're going to visit Pop, and then we can hang up your stockings."

"How will Santa know we're here though?"

"We can write him a note," Di said. "Now it must be bedtime."

Both kids protested loudly, even though Tate looked dead on his feet.

"We want her to read us a story," Lucy said, pointing to Mary.

"*Her* has a name," Di said, "and we didn't bring any books."

Lucy's face fell. "But we always have a story," she said.

"I could tell you a story?" Mary offered. Di looked at her with a grateful smile and both kids clambered up on the couch beside her.

"Tell us a Cwismas one," Tate said around the thumb in his mouth.

Mary thought for a minute. "Do you know the story about the magic peppermints?" she asked. Both kids shook their heads. Tate leaned in against her and she put her arm around his lovely warm pyjama-clad body. He was four, but he still had that lovely baby smell about him, fresh from the bath.

"Well, Christmas Eve is a very magical time," Mary said. "It's the only night of the year that you can grow candy in the garden."

Lucy looked at her dubiously. "Lollies come from the shops."

"Normally, yes," Mary said. "But not on Christmas Eve. Because if you plant a peppermint in the garden on Christmas Eve, do you know what happens?" Both kids shook their heads. "Well, when Santa's sleigh flies over the house, little bits of the magic that helps it fly sprinkle off and land on the ground. In the garden, the magic goes into the dirt and makes the peppermints grow. Do you know what they grow into?" Tate was almost asleep, growing heavier against her, but Lucy was wide eyed.

"What?" she whispered.

"Candy canes."

Lucy looked over at her dad. "Is that true?"

He shrugged. "This is the first I've heard of it. I guess you'll have to try."

Lucy slid off the couch and stood in front of her dad. "Can we do it now?"

"It has to be when Santa comes, so you'll have to wait until tomorrow. Maybe, since Uncle Bright doesn't have a very big garden, you could plant them at your pop's house?" Mary suggested. "And then you can all see what happens."

"Okay," Lucy said. "Will you do it with me?"

CHAPTER 35

According to the Dutch, hanging stockings comes from the custom of leaving shoes packed with food for Saint Nicholas's donkeys. He would leave small gifts in return. Another legend claims we hang stockings by the chimney because one year a poor widowed man didn't have enough money for his three daughters' dowries, making it difficult for them to marry. Saint Nick dropped a bag of gold down their chimney one night and into the freshly washed stockings the girls had hung by the fire to dry.

Bright

Klaus had been thrilled to see Bern, Di and the kids. It was a relief, Bright had to admit, that he had recognised them. He had wondered if his dad might get confused, especially with the twin thing.

As kids, they had tried to trick their parents numerous

times, but never succeeded. They'd had more luck at school, with teachers and other kids. Their best switch had been with Di though, when she and Bern had first started dating. It took her almost twenty minutes to work out that Bright had swapped places with Bern at the movies, although, to be fair, it was dark.

These days there were more obvious differences between them, and they were no longer in school uniforms either. Bern was a far more casual dresser, and a little bit fuller in the waist now too.

"So, Dad," Bern said after they'd had a cup of tea, "I hear you have a secret workshop."

Klaus took them into the garage and Bern stood looking around, an expression of sadness on his face.

"I'm having a few technical issues with the transport," Klaus said. "I could do with some help."

The 'sleigh' looked like it was made from pallets. One was probably from the bulk order of mince pies, Bright would guess. Klaus had been a carpenter in his day so he'd made a pretty good job of it. The swan-like back and seat looked sturdy. But it was sitting flat on the ground and wasn't going to move, magic or otherwise.

"This isn't bad, Dad," Bern said, giving his dad an affectionate pat on the shoulder. "How about we finish it off?"

Bright gave him a long look. "What are you doing?" he hissed.

Bern shrugged. "Look, it only needs a base and a coat of

paint and the kids will love it. What else am I going to do today? Plus it might be fun."

Bright looked between his brother and his dad. They used to make lots of things with their father as children, even the wooden garage Klaus must have forgotten, and Bern was right, it had been fun. "What the hell, why not?" he shrugged. "What do we need?"

They spent several hours sanding, nailing and glueing, and then they painted it red. The end result was pretty impressive. "You know, if we got one of the house trailers from work, this would be pretty cool to tow for a parade," Bright said. "Maybe next year I could see if anyone wants it."

He'd been at his dad's all morning, so he popped up to the office to check in, and maybe catch Mary too.

He found Dougal first. He was sitting at the baby grand piano, his back straighter than Bright had seen it, playing a beautiful rendition of 'Silent Night'. It sounded incredible.

Mary was in the main room with a handful of residents, putting on tablecloths and setting places. Lois was directing Bets on where to put some sort of candle decorations. Glenda was there, handing around pieces of Christmas cake. Bright was glad Klaus hadn't smelt it out like a bloodhound.

"You'll have a piece, won't you, Bright?" Glenda said, thrusting a napkin at him with a wedge of cake in it, the white icing sticking to the thin paper.

"Oh, I'm not much of a ..."

"But you have to," Glenda insisted. "It's Christmas Eve

and you have to make a wish on it."

Bright had never heard of that tradition. He surveyed the cake in his hand, eyeballing the dreaded almond icing.

"You never told me about the wish thing, Glenda," Mary said, coming over to stand next to him. "Do you mind, Bright?" She lifted the cake slice and took a large bite off the top, leaving only the fruitcake behind. She gave Bright a wink and then screwed shut her eyes, her hands in prayer, and made a wish.

He ate the rest of the cake and made a silent wish himself.

❄

Buddy was asleep in Bright's chair when he got to the office, but was happy enough to be picked up and placed on Bright's lap to finish his nap.

He didn't have much left to do, only a couple of last-minute payments. Janice popped her head around the corner to say goodbye. "Hope you've got your costume sorted for the party," she said with a wink. "See you tomorrow."

Bright sat and thought for a minute. He really wasn't a dressing up sort of guy. But he'd bet good money Mary was. He thought about her face at the skating rink and again when she told the kids about the candy canes, then he typed something into the search on his laptop, fishing in his pocket for his wallet to retrieve his credit card. What the hell, it was Christmas after all.

The clubhouse was closed until the party now and he was about to leave when he heard a strange noise coming from the cafe kitchen. On closer inspection, he discovered Mary, singing away badly, standing at the kitchen bench crying.

"Mary, what's going on?" he said, going in to comfort her. She looked up and grinned, her Christmas tree earrings swaying.

"Onions," she laughed. "I'm making stuffing. Want to help?"

She told him about the kids planting the peppermints while they worked. Bright chopped fresh herbs while she cracked eggs into a bowl. "They were so cute, they insisted on planting one for everyone, even the cat." She poured breadcrumbs into her stuffing mix. "Luckily, your dad had a big bag of candy canes for Bern to plant once they go to bed."

The stuffing done, they washed their hands under the tap, Bright leaning in to smell her.

"You have something, maybe red paint, on your wrist." She rubbed at the paint with her fingers. Her hand felt warm when she touched him.

"I missed you today," he said, and she turned to him.

"I missed you too."

He leant in and kissed her. She kissed him back and then he lifted her up, sitting her on the bench, and her legs went around his waist.

"This can't be hygienic," she said with a laugh when they caught their breath.

With a jarring, shockingly high-pitched squeal, the alarm went off.

"What the hell?" Bright said, and then the sprinklers turned on.

THE NEWSIE

Happy holidays, Merry Christmas and a very Happy New Year to all.

Have a wonderful festive season.

It'll be work as usual from 3 January.

CHAPTER 36

Mary

For a few seconds it was almost romantic. It was like being in the rain, in a movie. Mary still had her legs wrapped around Bright and their hair was wet, her clothes were soaked through. So was Bright's shirt.

Then he took her hand and helped her off the counter. "Come on, we need to get out of here."

"But the turkeys ... I need to get them stuffed ..." Mary started dumbly.

"Mary, there could be a fire somewhere. We need to check everyone's out and get outside ourselves."

The stuffing was now drowned in a puddle of water. She'd have to start over again. Together they went into the adjoining main lounge. It was a disaster zone. Everything was saturated. Her lovely table settings were ruined, the paper decorations on the tree hung limp and soggy, wine glasses either were filling with water or had fallen and smashed against each other.

They crossed the sodden carpet.

"I'll check the rec room and pool and you do the library and cinema," Bright said. "Check the bathrooms too, then we'll meet outside at the car park."

Beyond the foyer, the sprinklers hadn't been activated but the alarm blared. Mary called out and found nobody. There was no smoke or sign of a fire, so after doing a thorough check of her side of the building she went outside. A siren sounded somewhere nearby. Bright came out shortly afterwards.

"There's nobody inside and I can't see any sign of a fire," he said.

There was a sprinkling of dark chest hair visible through his wet shirt. Mary glanced down and was glad she was still wearing her apron.

"Nothing on my side either. Is that a fire engine I can hear?"

Bright nodded. The siren sounded closer. Some of the residents had gathered on the edge of the lawn to watch the drama unfold. Bright went over to talk to them and Mary watched as a red fire truck pulled slowly into the driveway.

Once it was confirmed that there was no fire and the sprinklers were turned off, they went back inside to survey the damage. It was bad. The carpet would need to be pulled up and replaced. Hopefully the chairs could be dried out, or they'd need to be replaced too. Red streaks bled across the tablecloths of the serving tables where the crepe paper flowers she'd made had been sitting. Now they were a pile of mush.

Mary started to pull the dripping decorations from the tree.

"Don't worry about that now," Bright said, coming up behind her and placing a hand on her shoulder. "We can sort it out later."

"There's not much time," Mary said, snivelling a bit. "I've got to redo the stuffing and dry all this lot out and find some more decorations for the tree ..." She burst into tears.

Bright wrapped his arms around her while she sobbed. "It's all ruined," she said. "There's hardly any time and there's already so much to do and it's going to look ... awful."

"Mary, it's fine. The insurance will cover most of it. We won't be able to use this room for a while but most of the activities ..."

"This is the only room that's big enough to hold the party." She pulled away to look up at him. He'd completely missed the point.

"The party?" Bright looked bewildered. "We can't have the party now."

"What do you mean we can't have the party? It's Christmas tomorrow. We can't not have the party."

"Look around you. Are you going to suggest everyone

wears gumboots?"

"We've always held Christmas here. All of the residents who are coming have nowhere else to go. Some of them have family coming." Anger had started to bubble up inside her.

"None of the houses have been affected. They can host their families there. The food is all okay, right? Aside from the stuffing."

"It won't be the same. They all love getting together for the party. It's become a tradition."

"Not this year. We'll set up a table in the rec room and the residents can come up and get what they need and take it back home." Bright started to gather up the broken wine glasses.

"Wow, that sounds cheery. We don't even get to eat to-gether. Lovely for the likes of Dougal and Lois who don't have anybody to spend the day with."

"It's just a day. You're making more of a drama about it than is necessary."

"It's not just a day." Mary refrained from stamping her foot like a toddler. Like Lucy had when she hadn't wanted to leave her pop's house earlier. "It's Christmas Day. And I'm *not* 'making a drama about it'. As usual, you're acting like a Grinch."

"You can't control everything." He stood, glaring at her, hands on hips. The frown lines were back. "Sometimes, things don't turn out to be rainbows and flowers. It's all very well being Miss Pollyanna and expecting life to be perfect.

Don't you find it fucking exhausting?"

Mary stared down at the soggy pile of streamers. She looked around at the room, which was completely unusable. And, shit, Dallas's equipment. It was wrecked.

"Maybe if we put half the tables in the rec room, and some in the foyer ..." But she knew it wouldn't work. She felt completely dejected. And angry. "Well, I guess this suits you, doesn't it?" she said, "Cheap and uncheerful. Just like you wanted." She took off her apron and shoved it into Bright's chest. "Merry fucking Christmas then." She was crying again, in that way she always did when she got mad.

"Look, I'm sorry, but ..."

"No, you're right. This isn't going to work." As she walked out the door, she wasn't sure if she meant the party, or them, or both.

Bright didn't follow her. She got on her bike and rode home, her shoes squelchy and her heart broken.

CHAPTER 37

In the movie How the Grinch Stole Christmas, the prosthetics and makeup Jim Carrey wore took three hours every day to put together. They were so miserable to apply and wear that Carrey consulted a Navy SEAL who taught him torture-resistance techniques.

Bright

He felt like an arsehole.

Mary had looked at him like he'd told her Santa Claus wasn't real. He wasn't sure she would ever talk to him again, or forgive him. He looked around the room in dismay, wondering where to start.

He'd have to ring the insurance broker, and ring a drainage company to get the surface water off. Then get hold of a carpet layer, which might prove tricky at this time of the year. The piano was probably ruined too, and Dallas's gear.

The firefighters had suggested it might have been a fault in the electrics causing excessive temperature that set the sprinklers off, so he needed to have that looked at too.

The party was really the last thing he needed to worry about.

Except he couldn't stop thinking about the look on Mary's face. How much she loved Christmas and how hard she'd worked. And how he thought maybe he had some pretty serious feelings for her. Was there any way to make the party work? Not inside, there wasn't. And you couldn't trust the weather on Christmas Day in New Zealand to stay dry enough to have an outdoor party without some sort of cover.

Something niggled in his mind. Then an idea started to form.

A cat meowed down the hallway and Buddy appeared, soaking wet and looking pissed off. Bright took one of the less soggy napkins off the table and used it to dry the cat off as best as he could.

"Poor Buddy," he said as Buddy purred. "When Bern goes, you can come and live with me. But first, we have to create some Christmas magic."

He started making some calls.

It was almost midnight before Bern, Gary and Dallas left. Bright stood and surveyed everything they'd managed to accomplish. It looked pretty good. It would be even better once they turned on the snow machine. The guy at the skating rink had been thrilled when Bright had turned up there ten minutes before closing, wanting to buy it. He'd even thrown in the archway for them to use, and the blow-up candy canes.

Gary had given them his marquee. They'd set it up on the lawn, placing it near the kitchen's casement window so they could pass the food out and avoid having people walking through the building. It was just big enough to fit all the tables under it and they'd dragged out all the plastic outdoor chairs from the storage shed and tied ribbons around them. Di had rounded up Lois and Bets to help and they'd thrown the tablecloths into their dryers. Glenda and Jerry had dried all the glasses and plates and the tables had been reset.

Dallas had been really good about the ruined deejaying gear, shrugging it off as 'one of those things'. The insurance would cover it, but it could take a bit of time. He'd also helped with getting the tent up, lugging furniture and mucking in. Bright owed him one.

Fairy lights had been strung up along the eaves of the building and the tree had been moved to the patio area. Bright had tried his best to remove all the soggy decorations and had even added some more from the box in Klaus's garage. He was hoping no one looked too closely at it.

Klaus's sleigh was now on a small trailer and they'd added shafts to allow them to harness the two ponies that were being dropped off in the morning. That had been the trickiest part, but Gary's mate had said his older daughter Tonya would come with the float and drive the makeshift cart for the right price.

The only thing he didn't have was music, but he was hoping he could use his mini speaker and play something from his phone. He was regretting now that he hadn't said yes to getting the jukebox fixed.

The whole thing was coming out of Bright's pocket, but it looked pretty good for a rush job. He hoped Mary would like it.

He wasn't sure what he would do if she didn't.

After a few hours of sleep, he got up to watch the kids open their presents and after breakfast he got dressed, wondering what the hell he had been thinking when he ordered his costume. Then he drove to Mary's.

CHAPTER 38

*Mariah Carey's classic hit 'All I Want for Christmas
Is You' is the number one holiday song that New
Zealanders like to have sex to.*

Mary

Mary had a terrible night's sleep and woke up for the first time in a long time not excited about Christmas. She felt bad for being so awful to Bright and blaming him for the party being ruined. It wasn't really his fault. And she couldn't expect everyone to love Christmas as much as she did.

Practically, she knew it wouldn't work to have the party at the clubhouse. Even if they had been able to fit everyone into the rec room, it would be a squeeze and they'd need to walk through the damaged lounge to the kitchen, which was probably considered a safety hazard. It was disappointing, that was all. She'd taken that out on Bright, when he was just trying to come up with a solution.

Christmas had always been important to her because of her gran but if Gran was here now, she'd have made the best of it. 'It's not how you react when life is easy, it's how you react when you've been dealt a dud hand', Gran would have said. The way Mary had reacted had been pretty poor.

She'd gotten up thinking that she would have to go around and apologise to Bright, so when he turned up at her house dressed as the Grinch, she thought she must still be dreaming. But there he stood, at her front door, wearing a red Santa jacket over green leggings that were two inches too short for his long legs and a green beard. He looked ridiculous. Mary's heart thumped erratically in her chest.

He held out the palm of his hand, encased in a green glove. There was a small gift-wrapped box in it. Inside was a pair of gaudy earrings. Little elves with pink hair and curly-toed shoes just like he had on.

"Before you say anything," he said, "please, come with me? I have something to show you. Bring your costume, you can change later."

It was amazing. Bright had completely transformed the Palms. Klaus was in his Santa suit, sitting atop a red sleigh being pulled by two dappled ponies, the grandkids sat next to him looking delighted. There was a layer of white snow on the back lawn. A marquee twinkled with lights and the tables were set with the stockings she had made at each setting.

"Merry Christmas, Mary," Bright said.

Bright helped her get the turkeys into the ovens, dress the salads and decorate the pavlovas. When everything was done, he popped a bottle of champagne and they sat outside in the sun to have a break.

"I can't believe you did all this," Mary said. The day was turning out beautifully, a light breeze blowing and the snow machine building up a layer of white to coat the lawn. "I'm sorry I was so awful yesterday."

"No, it's fine," Bright said. "I know how much the day means to you."

There was a wailing sound, and then a large pushchair emerged from around the side of the building. Andrew was looking frazzled, his wife Nat more put together. Mary leapt up to say hello and meet the babies.

"Over there, beside the door," Dougal said, coming around the corner. It took Mary a few minutes to realise it was him. He was in a tuxedo. Behind him, a couple of muscular guys she had never seen were struggling with an old piano. "That's it. Well done, boys, thank you." Dougal reached into his pocket and then gave them each a five-dollar note. They both looked bemused, then outright laughed when they saw

Bright in his costume. "Dale's sons," Dougal said as they left. "It might not be the best instrument, but it'll work."

Mary felt like she might cry. "Dougal, this is wonderful," she told him, giving him a hug. He gave her an awkward pat and then sat down to play.

Slowly all the residents began to arrive. Bets had on reindeer antlers and a red nose, Viv and Helen were in hilarious ugly sweaters. Glenda and Lois both turned up with angel halos much to their annoyance. Janice was an elf with bells on her shoes and pointy plastic ears. Slipping off to get changed into her Cindy Lou costume, Mary grinned as she clipped the big bow on her head, feeling happier than she had in a long time.

Everyone had a full glass when she got out and Bright made a toast. "Here's to Mary, our wonderful party organiser."

They all cheered.

Jerry arrived, a little flustered looking in his outfit. He was one of the wise men and he had a buttonhole pinned to his front. In one hand he had a bunch of matching pink roses and he placed them down in front of Lois with a little flourish.

"For you," he said. "Merry Christmas, Lois." She went the colour of the petals. So did Glenda as she scowled.

She'd hadn't made more stuffing, the Christmas puddings were a little bit of a disaster to look at, but tasted fine, and

Mary thought she'd never had such a wonderful Christmas Day.

"I can't believe you managed to pull this together," Andrew slurred in Mary's ear as they ate. "Especially after I screwed up the budget so badly."

"What do you mean?" she asked.

"Didn't Bright tell you? I undercharged some of the residents on some stuff. He didn't want to make a big deal about it to them and back charge them so he cut the Christmas budget instead." He hiccuped. "Not that you can tell, this all looks like it cost a bomb."

Klaus had taken most of the residents on a sleigh ride with Tonya steering them in a path around the lanes. Eventually Bright and Mary had a turn. Klaus had been very chatty with everyone as they perched up on the seat next to him, but he was quiet with Bright and Mary. They sat and held hands as they trotted along, stealing glances at each other and smiling.

"Wonderful. Thank you, Tonya. Thank you, Santa," Mary said as they got out.

Klaus looked around conspiratorially and then leant closer. "I don't know if I am really Santa," he whispered, looking worried. "I might be a bit mixed up."

Bright patted his knee. "You'll always be Santa for us, Dad," he said and Klaus beamed.

Mary looked at Bright in his hilarious green costume and thought, I think I might be in love with this guy.

Dougal had stopped playing, claiming he'd had enough and needed to get out of his monkey suit and away from the 'hordes'. Some people were helping to clean up, stacking up plates and scraping the scraps into a bucket for Tonya to take back for their pigs.

Mary went over to Bright and hugged him.

"You, Mr Nicols, are amazing."

There was a strange popping noise and then from inside, the old jukebox started to play 'All I Want for Christmas Is You'. Bright laughed and then they started to sway to the music, under the twinkling lights.

"Now that is a Christmas miracle," Mary said.

"No," Bright corrected her, "you are."

They kissed for a long time until someone in the background coughed. As they pulled apart, Mary noticed something from the corner of her eye.

"Oh my God, Bright. Are those the handcuffs on the tree?"

Epilogue

To: Andrew@Pacificpalms.com

Cc: AlbrightNicols@daintydwelings.com

Subject: Palms electrics

Hey mate,

Happy New Year.

Listen, I'm not sure how to tell you this, but I think I may have botched that job I did for you before Christmas.

Did you notice anything odd with things? Lights or anything?

Hopefully not, but I'll pop in when I get back from the break and have another look at it.

Sorry,

Dave

Gran's Christmas Pudding

This can be made up to three months ahead, but needs to be refrigerated.

You will need:

2½ cups sultanas or raisins

1½ cups currants

1 cup of other mixed, dried fruit, e.g. apricots, prunes, cranberries, glazed cherries

2/3 cup mixed peel

½ cup slithered almonds

½ cup brandy

a square of unbleached calico about 45 cm square

180 g butter

1 cup firmly packed brown sugar

5 eggs

¾ cup plain flour

½ cup self-raising flour

2 teaspoons mixed spice

2¾ cups breadcrumbs

3 cups finely grated suet

¼ cup extra brandy

string

Preparation:

Combine the fruit, nuts and brandy in a bowl, mixing well. Cover and let stand overnight or up to a week.

Soak the calico in cold water overnight. The next day, boil it for 20 minutes and rinse well.

Method:

Beat the butter and sugar in a large bowl with an electric mixer until just combined.

Beat in the eggs, one at a time, until just combined between additions.

Combine the egg mixture with the fruit mixture.

Add the sifted flour, spice, breadcrumbs and suet and the extra brandy and mix well.

Wearing rubber gloves to protect your hands, dip the calico cloth into a large pot of boiling water and wring out the excess water. Spread the cloth over the bench and rub in extra flour onto the cloth to cover most of it, thicker in the centre of the cloth, and leaving the edges bare.

Place your mixture into the centre of the cloth.

Gather the edges of the cloth together around the pudding. Hold up the pudding and pat it into a round shape. Tie the string securely around the top of the cloth, placing it as close to the pudding as possible to keep it firm. Tie a loop in the string at the top of the pudding, leaving the ends long.

You want the cloth as tight as possible to keep the pudding nice and round.

Carefully lower the pudding into the pot of boiling water (it should be about half full) and tie the string around the pot handles or to a wooden spoon across the pot to keep it from touching the base or sides. The pudding needs to be completely submerged.

Boil for approximately 6 hours, topping up the water as needed as it evaporates.

Remove the pudding, but do not set it down. Empty the water from the pot and then re-hang the pudding in the pot overnight.

The next day, place the pudding on the bench and cut the string. Loosen the cloth away from the top of the pudding and leave open to allow the cloth to dry (can be put in the fridge for this).

Once dry, re-tie the pudding and wrap or seal in a plastic bag and refrigerate until needed. Remove from the fridge 12 hours before eating.

On Christmas Day, boil the pudding in the same way for around 2 hours.

Remove from the water and suspend it for 10 minutes before cutting the string open and turning the pudding onto a serving plate and removing the cloth. Stand another 10 minutes before cutting.

Serve with brandy butter and custard, or dig a small well in the pudding, pour in brandy and light.

(Not Bright's) Eggnog

1½ cups milk

¾ cup cream

2 cinnamon sticks

1 vanilla bean pod, split open

1 teaspoon freshly grated nutmeg, plus more for garnish

3 eggs, separated

½ cup sugar

½ cup rum, bourbon or brandy

In a saucepan, combine the milk, cream, cinnamon, vanilla and nutmeg. Bring to the boil over a medium heat. Once it starts boiling, remove it from the heat and let cool.

Beat the egg yolks and sugar until well combined. Slowly whisk in the milk mixture until the mixture is well combined and smooth. Add the alcohol.

Refrigerate overnight or for up to 3 days.

Before serving, beat the egg whites until soft peaks form and fold them into your eggnog mix. Garnish with freshly grated nutmeg and serve.

Mary's Coconut Ice

2 1/3 cups icing sugar

1/4 teaspoon cream of tartar

395 g can sweetened condensed milk

3 1/2 cups desiccated coconut

2 teaspoons vanilla essence

red or pink food colouring

Grease a square cake pan. Line the base and sides with baking paper, extending the paper slightly above the edges of the pan.

Sift the icing sugar and cream of tartar together into a large bowl. Add sweetened condensed milk, coconut and vanilla. Mix until well combined. Divide mixture in half. Tint half the mixture pink with food colouring. Leave the other half plain.

Press the plain mixture over the base of your prepared pan, levelling the top with the back of a spoon. Press the pink mixture over the plain mixture, levelling the top with your spoon. Cover. Chill for 3 hours or until set.

Cut the coconut ice into small squares.

Serve.

This will keep for up to a month.

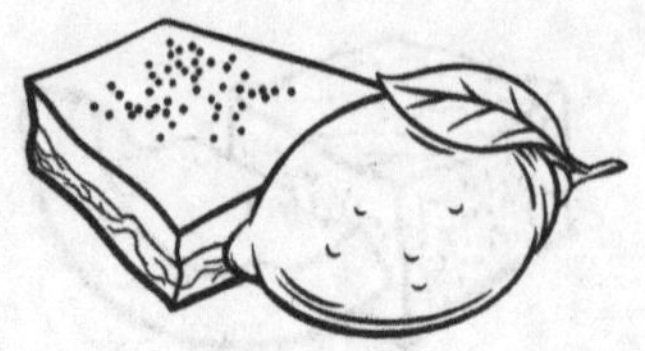

Glenda's Famous Lemon Slice

For the base:

150 g unsalted butter, melted

1/2 teaspoon vanilla extract

1/3 cup caster sugar

1 1/3 cups plain flour

1 tablespoon cornflour

For the top:

4 eggs

1 teaspoon finely grated lemon rind

1/3 cup plain flour

1 1/3 cups caster sugar

2/3 cup lemon juice

icing sugar to serve

Method:

Preheat the oven to 180°C.

Grease a large slice pan. Line with baking paper, allowing a small overhang on all sides.

Mix the melted butter, vanilla and sugar. Sift in the flour and cornflour. Using a wooden spoon, stir until a soft dough forms. Press into the pan. Bake for 15 to 20 minutes or until golden. Remove from the oven and let cool.

Whisk the eggs, lemon rind, flour and sugar together until smooth, then add the lemon juice. Pour this over the base. Bake for 15 minutes or until just set.

Cool completely in the pan.

Cut into pieces, dust with icing sugar and serve.

About the authors

Nikki and Kirsty are sisters from New Zealand.
They love travelling, reading, Harry Styles and great food.
Neither of them can do a cartwheel for love nor money.

www.nikkiperryandkirstyroby.com

www.ingramcontent.com/pod-product-compliance
Lightning Source LLC
Chambersburg PA
CBHW011322310726
48973CB00011B/3020